LET BYGONES BE BYGONES

BONNER LITCHFIELD

LET BYGONES BE BYGONES

Jane felt Peter's back arch with each stroke of her index finger. She knew she shouldn't have a favorite. It just felt wrong. But despite being the most temperamental creature she'd ever encountered, it was moments like these that Jane cherished. She didn't care that he was kneading her threadbare couch. His loud purr relaxed her very soul.

Of course, she cared for the others too. Hilda, Sofie, Rhubarb, Dustin, and Julian. Each of them had made the grade, after all. Countless others hadn't been up to snuff. And they'd had to go. No guilt, no remorse. Jane couldn't keep them. Not in this crazy age where the monthly fee for a single pet exceeded the cost of supporting two children. And unlicensed ownership was unthinkable. Jane smiled at the thought. Unthinkable, unless you planted your own microchip in the select few.

Peter jumped off the couch and disappeared—two seconds before the doorbell rang. Jane glanced at her wall display for the front porch camera and sighed. Then she got up and opened the door to a pudgy man in a gray uniform.

The badge on his chest identified him as Agent Randy Wright. Animal control. "Ms. Breckenridge?"

"Yes. Please call me Jane."

"I've just captured an unauthorized cat right here on this block."

Jane bit her lip. "I see ... well, thank you."

"Got him right here. Need for you to take a look."

"I'm afraid I don't understand," Jane said. But she understood all too well. The wire cage, slightly larger than a breadbox, and the cat stuffed inside it gave her way too much info.

"I need for you to look at this cat and see if you can identify the owner," Agent Wright snapped.

A transparent ploy. Jane knew full well that she was his prime suspect. "What makes you think there's an owner?" she asked.

"Because he's well fed and his fur's not matted. This one's been cared for by somebody. Say! I'll ask the questions here."

Jane forced herself to smile. "Very well, young man. Let's have a look." She leaned forward, using her cane for support. "Oh my, this one looks like a troublemaker."

"Have you seen him before?"

Seen him? The sight of Julian in the cage was ripping her heart out. Jane focused on keeping her voice mildly curious. "He looks familiar. Give me a minute."

"Give you a minute. Right. You bygones are worthless. Sponging off the rest of us. No good for anything else. Why don't you do us all a favor and die?"

Okay. That didn't take long. Less than sixty seconds on the verbal abuse. Oh, wouldn't she love to poke that fat pig's eyes out with the tip of her cane! Not an option. The next best thing was to appear vulnerable and weak. So Jane dropped her emotional resistance, allowing tears to leak from her eyes. This clod would think that his cutting remarks had upset her. Not at all. Her tears were for ...

Julian! He let out a pitiful yowl that made Jane want to scream. She couldn't let him be taken. *Don't be silly,* she chided herself. *He's not up to snuff.* But hadn't he responded to his training at a very high level? Easily cracked the top one percentile of her test group.

Suddenly, Jane clutched her chest. So much for caution and prudence! Her cane clattered on the concrete stoop. Lurching forward, she grabbed a handful of Agent Wright's collar. "Can't ..." She gasped.

"What the hell." The fat man stiffened.

"Help ..." Letting herself go limp, Jane fell against Agent Wright. She closed her eyes and let her neck become rubber. Her head flopped against his chest. It was early spring in the suburbs. Warm and sunny, but not unpleasant. But this fat pig absolutely reeked of sweat.

Wright shoved her to the ground and backed away as if old age, bygone-ism, was a contagious illness. Not too long ago, behavioral norms dictated that he break her fall out of pure instinct. But they were living in a new era with a different set of standards. This is what public servants had digressed to ... sociopaths with underdeveloped morals.

Jane landed with a thud. This was going to hurt tomorrow. Assuming she could get up. Old fool. Risking injury to save Julian. So unfair to the others.

Meanwhile, her cat yowled and clawed against the cage. Jane was sobbing now. No reason to mask her emotions at this stage of the game.

Then, through her blur of tears, Jane saw a cute young couple that lived down the street from her. The Millers. These two would have been called yuppies in her day—a much nicer label than bygone. They were pushing a baby carriage, strolling along if this whole scene between her and Agent Wright was nothing more than a mirage. An old person manhandled on her front porch, and they hadn't even paused out of curiosity. Human behavior certainly had changed during the past twenty years.

"There!" Jane pointed a crooked finger at the Millers.

"What are you babbling about now?" Agent Wright asked.

"Them. They're the cat's owners. I saw them, I tell you. They were feeding that disease-carrying vermin. I told you I'd remember if you gave me half a chance."

Agent Wright straightened his collar and mopped his self-important face with a handkerchief. "You expect me to believe a single word that comes out of your mouth?"

"They've got a cat in their baby buggy. Another one! It's happening right under your nose, and you're too damned blind and conceited to notice."

Agent Wright scowled down at Jane. Then he stepped down off her porch and took a couple of hesitant steps towards the Millers. He stopped when Ms. Miller bent over and took a baby out of the carriage.

Meanwhile, the cage had a sliding door secured by a simple latch. Jane only needed a moment. By the time Agent Wright turned around, Julian was gone. A black and white streak of disappearing calico cat.

Wright's face was beet red. "You did this," he sputtered.

Jane ignored him. She was pleased to get herself to a sitting position without undue effort. "You're lucky I'm not hurt."

"Like anybody cares. Bygone."

"They might care that you don't know how to set a

proper latch. That cat pushed the cage door open just as easy as you please."

That got him. Agent Randy Wright snatched up the empty cage. "You best keep all of this to yourself," he said. "Or I'll make your life a living hell. Bygone! You hear what I'm saying to you?"

Jane smiled. "I hear you quite clearly," she said. "And thank you for your service. Cat catching's a proud calling."

"At least I've got a job." The man sneered. "And a life."

"And a fine one it is," Jane said. "Say, I don't suppose you'd mind helping an old woman up to her feet ..."

The Animal Control agent stomped off. Jane waited until he drove away before standing up on her own. One advantage of old age was appearing to be more helpless than she really was. Of course, that didn't outweigh the liability of being a second-class citizen.

But no time for dwelling on social injustice. Jane went inside and launched an app on her tablet—her own creation, not available for public download—and chose the menu option to summon everybody. Hilda emerged from under the bed, Sofie from behind the couch. Rhubarb entered through the rear window. All of them were too smart to be seen until Jane summoned them. *What had gone wrong with Julian?* Something to figure out later. Right now, the Millers had left their house unattended.

TWENTY MINUTES LATER, the cats were relishing their reward, a beef and tuna fish concoction guaranteed to make the taste buds dance with glee. They'd done well. Another successful mission. Executed with their usual combination of teamwork and stealth.

Jane pried up a floorboard in the back corner of her closet and added the gold bracelet to her secret stash. Ms. Miller was an attractive young woman with expensive tastes. And her husband obviously knew about keeping her happy. The bracelet would fetch a pretty penny through channels that Jane used to sell her wares.

"Imagine," she said to herself. "There was a time when I thought of the dark web and black market as pure evil. Now they've become my neighborhood. Welcome to the underbelly of society, Doctor Jane Breckenridge." Jane smiled and shook her head. She hadn't spoken her former title, "Doctor," out loud in a long time. Why would she? It was a relic from a former life that no longer existed.

But enough of that. She was squandering quality time with these pointless musings. She was curled up with her cats on a lumpy mattress in the rear bedroom. Dustin's purr was loud as a vacuum cleaner. And Peter's warmth against Jane's leg radiated down to her feet.

Poor Julian! Off sulking in a corner. All alone. Just him and his injured pride. Upset that he didn't get to participate in the mission at the Miller house. Well, he'd have to stay mad for a while. At least until Jane figured out what had gone wrong with him. Which gave her pause. If a smart cookie like Julian got himself captured by a first-class ninny like Agent Randy Wright, something was definitely amiss.

For now, though, leisure time with her darlings was top priority. Hard to believe ... there was a period in her life when she considered animals to be nothing more than tools and building blocks in the field of cognitive psychology—same as molecules in chemical engineering. And Jane had run the research gamut with lab rats, and then monkeys.

The cats came later. Cats! Smart, creative, exceptional memory, long attention span. But also fiercely independent.

In fact, conventional wisdom considered cats to be untrainable. Especially when it came to doing tricks or obeying commands ...

But their contrariness was what made them special. Which was, in fact, the whole point of her field of study. Teaching the unteachable. Using an uncooperative subject's eccentricities as a vehicle for behavior modification. Too bad, she never found a way to make it work with humans.

Suddenly, the cats disappeared. All six of them. Including Julian.

Jane's breath caught in her throat. The scientist in her wondered why she was startled or surprised. She'd conditioned this behavior in them, after all.

Then someone beating on her front door ... also not unexpected, given her cat's preemptive reaction.

She switched her wall display to the camera under the front porch eave and gritted her teeth. Agent Wright was there with another man in uniform. What the hell ... people of his ilk didn't work overtime. He should be home watching sitcoms and stuffing his fat face with junk food.

Willing herself calm, Jane picked up her cane and wrapped a shawl around her shoulders even though she wasn't cold. The knocking got louder. Jane arranged her face into an expression of good-natured bewilderment and opened the door. "Why hello. Can I help you?"

"You've got some serious explaining to do," Agent Wright said.

"You woke me," Jane protested and feigned a shiver. "I don't understand."

"Cut the crap."

The other agent cleared his throat. "Hello, Ms. Breckenridge. I'm Agent Gregory Scott."

"Oh my," Jane said. "Am I in some sort of trouble?"

"Not at all." Agent Scott, a fresh-faced man in his forties, held up a hand to silence Wright. "I just need to ask ... well, you wouldn't know anything about an illegal cat. No. Of course not."

Jane offered up a self-effacing laugh. "Know anything? I barely remember what I ate for breakfast this morning," she said.

It was dark outside. The surrounding trees in the neighborhood had become a shadowy web. And this Agent Scott, obviously Wright's superior, was the spider. He was staring at Jane with searching green eyes, luring her in, offering a false sense of security. Ready to ensnare her—the slightest mistake on her part would do the trick.

Scott continued in his soothing voice. "The thing is ... well, there's this video." On his tablet, he replayed earlier footage from Jane's front porch and fast-forwarded to the point where she flipped the latch to release Julian.

Jane's knees became weak. An icy hand clutched at something inside of her—chilling her very core. She let a tear roll down her cheek. "That never happened," she said.

"Now, now."

"My heart ..." Jane said. "Now I remember! You realize, of course, that you'd be required to play the video in its entirety in court. Including the part where I had a dizzy spell and this fat prick shoved me to the ground."

Agent Scott spread his arms in a gesture of humility. "It won't come to that," he said. "And even if it did, the issue in question is *you* releasing an animal from our custody. That's a pretty serious charge. It would be a shame to see you lose your freedom and this cute little bungalow."

Jane sucked in her breath, masking both fear and disdain for the men on her porch. Agent Wright—stupid blob of jello that he was—had no clue. He was standing there, smug as a clam, not worried at all about the axe hanging over his head. Clearly, his boss had no problem showing video footage of him shoving an old woman, if that's what it took to make his case. And any consequences that he might suffer would be deemed acceptable.

Except ... they were really after something else. Their video of her opening the cage was enough to pin a charge on her. Yet, they hadn't arrested her. *They suspect more.*

"I understand what you're dealing with," Agent Scott said. "I really do. You've outlived all of your friends and you're lonely. Nobody would blame you for wanting to befriend a stray or two."

So that was it: actual pet ownership. Even so, this civil lackey was clueless to the extent of Jane's crimes—no, not crimes. Lifestyle! She was an anachronism adapting to the futuristic—albeit backward—world that had formed around her.

And they could pucker up and kiss her withered old ass. She didn't make the rules. She didn't write the legislation that put oldsters (bygones!) on the government teat and forced the working class to pay for those meager benefits. In fact, she'd still be pursuing her own career if she hadn't been unceremoniously forced out by age-specific mandates.

So enough! Enough cowering. Enough role playing. Enough portraying a meek and bewildered old ... Bygone. She was sick of this shit. Her voice became cold as flint. "Quit playing games. Tell me what the hell you want with me."

The agent flinched. No more Mister Smooth Talker. "This is way more of a break than you deserve: but if you'll admit to owning that cat you released this afternoon, admit ownership and turn the animal over to us, you won't face criminal charges. But if you make us hunt down that cat and force us to drag the truth out of you, it will go hard."

"That's a brilliant theory you've got there," Jane said. "Me. An old woman living alone who can barely support herself. Taking on a pet? Really!"

"Don't play that game," Agent Wright sneered. "I was onto you the second you opened your front door."

"Were you now? Okay. Yes. You've got me. You're just too smart. Give yourself a gold star, Agent Pork belly. You've just outwitted a bygone. In fact, let me call my cat for you right now. Kitty, kitty, kitty! Here, kitty! Well, I guess he's not coming. Wait! I'll show you a picture of him."

Leaving the front door open so those boobs wouldn't think she was trying to escape through a hidden tunnel, Jane went inside and got her tablet. On her way back, she issued a command on her app. Then she walked back outside to face the agents. "Well, here he is," she said. "A real threat to public safety." Her tablet displayed the cover of the old children's book, *Cat in the Hat*.

Wright's mouth hung open. Nostrils flaring, he clenched his fists till his arms trembled.

Agent Scott favored Jane with a wintery smile. "Thank you for your time," he said. "We'll be seeing you again. Real soon."

As they turned to leave, Jane's heart caught in her throat. First Julian had been careless. And now, Peter! He almost didn't get himself hidden in time. Something was definitely amiss.

That thought made Jane sick with worry. Too much angst to fully enjoy the sight of the livid Animal Control agents walking around their vehicle. Her babies worked fast. In seconds, they had let the air out of all four tires. All in response to the command she'd just sent.

FIVE WEEKS HAD PASSED.

It was midafternoon, bright and sunny outdoors. But Jane felt like a little girl who was afraid to turn off her night-light in the wee hours of an inky black night. She wore a floppy hat with a wide canvas brim to avoid surveillance. Face recognition and all of that. Not that it mattered now. She was just keeping up the appearance that nothing had changed.

Same as always, she stood in front of the grocery store, watching and waiting. Only this time, every approaching car made her squirm. She clutched the cloth grocery bag she'd had for years, twisting it in her hands; it was empty except for a few valuables hidden in the lining.

A respectable looking couple with two children in tow emerged from an oversized van. Her call to action.

But instead of following them inside, Jane sat down on a bench and waited. She'd give it ten minutes and not a single second more than that. Then what? Didn't matter. If they didn't hold up their end of the deal by 3:00 PM, they weren't going to honor it at all.

Animal Control was a joke. The same with traffic and litter enforcement. Even the Department of Personal Security—traditional law enforcement that dealt with real crime like theft and violence—was a pushover compared to ... *Them.* They were the reason for Jane's twisted gut and the taste of metal in her throat. She wasn't in the shallow end of the pool with the kiddies anymore. She'd taken a dive into the deep water where the sharks fed.

The first ping of her tablet made her jump. One minute to spare. By the time Jane opened the document, a second message was delivered. Jane looked at both documents, verified their authenticity with a pirated app, and saved copies of both to her black cloud account. Satisfied, she stood up, head bowed, shoulders stooped. Playing her role to the hilt. A blundering old bygone buying groceries on the taxpayer's dime.

IT HAD ALL GONE SMOOTH. Too smooth.

Jane got off the bus two blocks from her house. The conclusion of a successful shopping trip. She now had two encrypted documents on her tablet and on the cloud. Both had the federal government's binary e-seal, something that couldn't be forged, though countless hacker types had tried. The first document granted Jane immunity from prosecution in exchange for giving up her largest buyer.

Their exchange in the supermarket went exactly as planned. Why wouldn't it? Again, too smooth. The children, a boy and a girl, staged a row at the appropriate moment. Their grating wails made a root canal seem pleasant in comparison. With their mother trying to quiet them down and their father stomping down the aisle to reprimand them in a booming voice, nobody noticed that Jane added several of their peaches to her own shopping bag. Embedded inside one of the peaches was a microchip with the encoding for a ten-thousand-dollar e-credit. Meanwhile, the quarreling family had acquired Jane's latest haul, which included some rare heirloom jewelry. Not the best she'd ever sold, but quality stuff.

And now, after the fact, Jane couldn't help wondering what happened to that family after the exchange. Were they arrested the moment they stepped outside? Were they allowed to go on their merry way with zero consequences?

And if they'd been arrested, would they be prosecuted for the sake of keeping up appearances?

Because she'd pegged that family for undercover cops a long time ago. Why? Every exchange she'd ever had with them was problem free. Never a glitch. You almost always had to improvise a little or wait out a nosy surveillance drone that floated in unexpectedly, even when you thought you had the timing nailed. But with these people, everything always happened right on time with nary a hiccup. Unreality defined.

Boy had she ever gotten over on *Them*. The bastards! She had her signed documents, and she'd fulfilled her part of the deal by delivering a major buyer of stolen merchandise. As promised. How was she supposed to know she was setting up one of their undercover operatives ... Ha!

Of course, she feared retribution. Any sensible person would. So she checked in with herself. *Know what they say about high stakes games at your age? They say fuck it and get on with it!*

Jane took a deep, cleansing breath; she'd needed that personal pep talk. And it made sense. All she had was today —no really, from cradle to grave, all anyone had was the one unique day that *was* today. Live it or waste it. Those were her choices. Yeah. Those thoughts sounded good in theory. But that shit she'd just pulled was going to piss *Them* off in a big way.

Sighing, Jane gathered herself for the walk home. She could keep trying to convince herself she wasn't scared shitless. She could try ...

JANE APPROACHED her house in a cold sweat. Her heart was pounding like a trip hammer—probably at a dangerous intensity for someone her age. She reminded herself of the second document. The important one. The one that granted her unrestricted ownership of up to ten cats with no adoption fees or monthly pet tax. That meant Animal Control could stick it. Not that they'd ever been more than a mere annoyance in the first place.

So she had in her possession a binding contract, replete with all of the appropriate legalese. In particular, section 3, subparagraph A: *Will not kill, harm, or partake in any action with intent to wound or injure.* Guaranteed health and longevity for the cats.

Reassuring words on the surface. They'd stick to their agreement. Especially one with a federal e-seal. But Jane knew *Them.* They'd never rope themselves into a contract without leaving themselves a loophole. You could bet on that.

That's why she came home to seven wicker baskets lined up on her front porch. Even though she'd already anticipated something along these very lines, Jane sat down on the bottom step. Her chest ached as if a goddamned elephant was sitting on it!

Pull yourself together fool! Get everyone inside.

Willing herself to stand, Jane opened her front door and carried each basket into her bedroom. So hard to detach— and that's what had caused this mess in the first place. Attempting behavior modification on subjects you'd bonded with catapulted *stupid* to a whole new stratosphere.

Back to the terms spelled out in her second encoded document ... the 'no harm' section contained an additional clause: *will not be subjected to any unpleasant stimuli.* Well, they'd kept their word. Six baskets, six sleeping cats. All completely unharmed. And not the least bit uncomfortable. In fact, every one of them was purring loud. Enjoying a long, pleasant nap that they'd never wake up from. That was the catch. Their coup de grâce. They hadn't hurt or maimed them. Instead, they'd given them permanent naps that were actually pleasant. And no, the naps wouldn't kill them—as long as Jane maintained intravenous feedings— they'd just never awaken.

The seventh basket contained a syringe with a bright red ribbon wrapped around it. A special gift for Jane. One injection for a human-sized perma-nap. An easy way out if she chose to take it. *She* was their end game. Not the cats. Not the rash of larceny in her neighborhood. Their true objective was elimination of a bygone. Scraping a parasite off the skin of society.

So Jane sat in her rocker, arms folded, tablet in her lap. The baskets arranged in a semicircle around her. Six sleeping cats. They wouldn't wake up if you fired a gun or blasted a trumpet. A mouse could scamper from one basket to the next and they'd never stir.

She'd trained them well. Seeing them curled up and relaxed, hearing their deep contented purrs, watching their paws knead the foam padding, you'd never know they were faking it. Or maybe they weren't. That's why Jane couldn't bring herself to launch the app on her tablet.

Riddled with doubt, Jane reshuffled recent events in her head. A delay tactic. A coward's avoidance. Yet, she indulged herself just the same.

It hadn't been easy. The lab equipment in her pantry was a joke compared to the state-of-the-art facility where she used to work. And there'd been risk involved. Every outside venture for her babies had been a gamble. No guarantee that any of them would make it back before their abilities were unduly compromised.

But eventually, after several carefully orchestrated outdoor excursions, Jane found traces of the tranquilizer, meprobamate, in their bloodstream. It was combined with a molecular structure that she couldn't identify. Apparently, this mystery compound slowed and prolonged the sedative effect, causing symptoms to appear later and last longer.

At that point, she'd been forced into a detached clinical approach that sickened her. But she did it. Choking back sobs, Jane fed Peter a concoction that made him puke. No trace of the drug in his vomit, thus ruling out food and water as the delivery mechanism. A series of skin grafts followed. And that process also brought Jane to tears. Shaving part of their fur. Scraping skin samples from different areas.

Finally, after several weeks of this grueling guessing game, Jane knew. The cats had ingested the toxin through their paws. Simple but effective. Spray a wide area. And the cats were bound to walk through it at some point.

Not hard to connect the dots from there. They'd discovered a pattern of thefts—not break-ins or burglaries, but valuables just going missing in households in a three-mile radius. Maybe a camera had detected a cat or two. Nothing suspicious in itself. In fact, the police wouldn't give it a second glance. But *They* had people whose entire existence was ferreting out the hidden truths behind things that were probably nothing.

The tranquilizer spray on the ground had been a trap for Jane, not the cats. And she'd stumbled right into it. From a due diligence standpoint, she should have been taking blood samples from her subjects on a regular basis. Instead, she became a liability, a weak link in a chain. Because at some point, the cats went from being subjects to pets. Once that happened, she told—no deluded!—herself that it wasn't necessary to subject them to the discomfort of a pinprick. And had nearly wound up getting them captured and euthanized.

Back to Animal Control ... if they'd managed to take Julian and bust Jane for unauthorized ownership of him, *they* probably wouldn't have explored the home larceny angle any further. But after she made those morons look even dumber than cat excrement ...

It all came down to this moment. Had she played it right? In theory, yes. The facts lined up. Her strategy was sound. The polymer coating she'd applied to the cat's paws would keep that damn tranquilizer from touching them. Unless they were one step ahead of her—maybe saturating the air, or just shooting the cats with darts. No. Jane had given no sign that she was onto them. She'd guessed right. Her strategy was sound.

If you could overlook the fact that she'd become the weak link. The one who almost got them all killed. A sentimental old bygone. Too emotionally attached to pull her head out of her ass.

Gritting her teeth, Jane fired up her app and issued the command to wake them up. No. Not wake them up. To let them know they could quit playing dead now.

Only they didn't move. Not a flicker of an eyelid. Not a twitch of a paw. Six purring cats, sound asleep ... for the rest of their lives.

Jane let out a huge groan of despair. She stood up and paced the room, fighting the urge to smash her tablet against the wall. Couldn't do that. There was no other way to ping the cat's embedded microchips and tell them, "Wake up; the coast is clear." So destroying the tablet would be the same as taking a loved one off of life support.

Even though, sometimes, letting someone go was the merciful thing to do. Yes. Merciful. Jane picked up the syringe. It would be simple, quick, and painless. All she had to do was touch the orange grommet to any part of her body and press the black button. She'd be unconscious long before the cats faded into eternal slumber.

No! This could not happen. She'd tested and retested the polymer coating that she'd applied to their paws. She'd coached them on where to go and when to go there. She'd even done a couple of dry runs with Hilda and Sofie through known contaminated areas. It had to work.

Maybe they'd switched compounds. Or upped the dosage. Or used another method ...

No. She'd given *Them* no reason to suspect their net wasn't airtight. Nothing had changed.

Jane relaunched the app and reissued the wakeup command, screaming in frustration. It *had* to work.

She closed her eyes ... took a deep breath ... tilting her head back, she emptied her mind of all things irrelevant. The fact that she'd maybe killed her babies—she hadn't! This had to work—stop. Irrelevant! None of this mattered. What mattered was why. Nothing else.

What unknown variable was in play here? Not the staged bust at the supermarket, not the encoded federal agreement docs, nor the polymer coating on the cat's feet. Certainly not the cat's training. They were rock solid. It all came down to her. What had she overlooked? What had she done to foul things up? What was she not seeing?

"Oh ... of all the silly things." She'd been so intent on pouring over the verbiage in the documents and the myriad of other details that she'd blanked out on the simple and obvious. *Her tablet was offline.* The message they used to send the documents could have a Trojan ... No. She'd just touched something she shouldn't have. Weak link. Living up to her self-dubbed moniker. Hands trembling, Jane brought her tablet back online and executed the wakeup command once more.

Six cats sprang out of their baskets. Their bright eyes fastened on Jane, awaiting instructions.

She collapsed to her knees into the middle of them. "Come here. Oh, Peter, Julian, Rhubarb. Come here. All of you!"

Six purring cats, one delirious old bitty with tears streaming down her cheeks. Relief washed over her. Joyous relief.

"Peter, no!"

The large white tomcat had the syringe. It wasn't like him to play with foreign objects without permission.

"Put that down," Jane said.

Then she knew. He was responding to another command. That plunger was still meant for her. She looked at the cats. A dozen bright eyes staring her down. Suddenly, she was very afraid.

Peter stood on his hind legs with the syringe between his front paws. Touching the orange grommet to the wall, he injected the lethal compound into the wood and plaster. Then he pranced across the room and wound himself around Jane's legs.

"Thank you, Peter." Jane stroked his fur and sighed.

But it wasn't over. Nobody intentionally pissed off ... *Them.* Oh, well. They'd just have to let bygones be bygones.

In the meantime, it was hard to rub six cats with only two hands. But she'd get around to them all. They had time. They had impunity.

OUSTED

Alex leaned against his van and squinted through his sunglasses at the snazzy house he was about to lose. Sharp brickwork, dormers jutting out of a steep roof. All of that said high dollar.

He should just crawl back into the van and leave here. Give it up. Lower his standards a little. But he couldn't stop staring at that house. At this whole damn neighborhood, with its shiny cars and green lawns. Everything was new here. Gleaming white driveways. Dark black rooflines.

And his next-door neighbor was cooking steaks again. You didn't get those smells in every neighborhood. Projects and trailer parks smelled of stale beer and car exhausts. There, you got canned goods for dinner—everything processed, preserved, and tasting like metal.

Then he saw it. In the front window of the house. A curtain moved. Someone looking out at him. It drew back again. Another quick look. Probably still in her pajamas. She did that when she was down. Alex didn't need to see inside to know: Lisa had that same scared look from last night. Now she was peeping at him from behind the window curtain, looking at him, then at the hole—that hole in the sheetrock that wasn't really his fault.

Alex opened the back door to his van. It was hard to find work when you drove a beat-up vehicle that sounded like it was going to shake apart. But with the money leaking out of their bank account—first for one dumb purchase, then a minor splurge—they had to cut back some kind of way. Besides, fixing things was what he knew.

And he could fix this. If Lisa would let him in. Give him a chance. Yeah, she had a right to be upset. Last night ... well, that was just a three-second shit-fit he'd been provoked into.

Alex grabbed a ten-inch square of plywood that he'd cut earlier and a scrap piece of sheetrock. He liked handling building materials. The splintery plywood, the smooth sheetrock. One for support, the other for looks. Everything he needed to patch that hole good as new. At least to start. There'd be paint to match later.

With the sheetrock and plywood tucked under his arm like a pair of school books, he reached for the cool metal handle of his toolbox. All he'd need out of there was his drill, his knife, and a few screws. But he liked to haul everything with him, just in case.

He made it three steps before the plywood clattered on the pavement. He dropped the toolbox too; it landed next to him with the sickening thud of metal hitting asphalt. Then Alex was holding his head with both hands, staggering sideways like a drunk fool. But he wasn't drunk. He'd been pop-Zapped.

LEAVE THE PREMISES.

Alex still hadn't recovered. Now they were giving him orders.

LEAVE THE PREMISES NOW.

That damn voice made his teeth rattle. Seemed like it put out enough vibration to split somebody's skull. And he had a metal taste in his mouth. Metal and blood. That's when he realized that he'd just bitten his tongue. Could be worse. Some people who got pop-Zapped had been known to piss in their pants. You might even puke up blood if you overstayed your welcome.

Alex gathered himself and staggered towards the van, then realized he was forgetting his toolbox. Had to go back for it. Didn't want to. But he needed it. Lurching forward, he bent to pick it up.

LEAVE THE PREMISES. YOU HAVE THIRTY SECONDS.

A woman was walking her dog. Right across the street from him. And she didn't even look his way. That booming command should have broken every window in the neighborhood, but not even a dog could hear it. Just Alex.

He looked up—scared to see them, even more scared to look away. There were three of them. Or maybe just one. Who knew what they really looked like? At any rate, he could see three transparent lines about ten yards away; they were hovering in the air at different heights. Every couple of seconds, they'd swap places with one another. At least it seemed that way. They reminded Alex of floating strips of clear tape.

TWENTY SECONDS.

He was moving now. Heaving his toolbox into the back of the van, not caring what spilled out. When he turned the key, the van spluttered into life, then went silent. The strong smell of gasoline told him the engine was flooded.

TEN SECONDS.

Dammit. He really needed to let it sit for five minutes. But that trio of assholes (or single asshole) wouldn't wait.

Slamming the gas pedal to the floor, he turned the key, only to get the labored chug of the engine turning over and not catching.

LEAVE NOW.

He jumped out of the van and barely remembered to shut the door before he took off running. Running flat out. Not even looking where he was going. Just hauling ass. Right away, it felt like there was a barbell pressing down on his chest. And his pants started chaffing his inner thighs. But as much as he wanted to get out of this hot sun and plop down under a shade tree, he could not stop, or even slow down. He wasn't getting pop-Zapped again.

ALEX SLOWED to a jog at the end of his cul-de-sac. He made it another hundred yards and had to walk.

Okay. They'd run him off from his own house. Probably because Lisa was still scared. There was no way to talk to them, but if she'd calm down and invite him back in, maybe they'd let things ride. *Sure. No problem. How the hell am I going to manage that?*

Sweat stung his eyes, blurring his vision. He heard the hum of an approaching vehicle and decided to just keep walking down the middle of the road. Not long ago, the driver would have laid on the horn and yelled. Or maybe just run you over. But ever since those damn beings (or whatever they were) had shown up and started interfering with people, payback for violent behavior was guaranteed.

This driver coasted to a stop and rolled down the window. "Hey, Alex. Are you alright?" It was Rachel Kip, who lived three houses down from him.

Alex thought fast. "Hey Rachel," he said. "You think

you could give me a lift home? My van's broke down and Lisa's not home right now. I was trying to walk to the store, but it's hotter out here than I thought."

"Well, alright," Rachael looked uncertain. "I guess."

She knew Alex as a neighbor, and she had no reason to worry about him assaulting her—not these days. But old instincts didn't just go away. Probably, the only reason he was getting this ride was that they were only a few hundred yards from home.

When he got in the front passenger seat, Alex shivered from the sudden transition from hot sun to ice cold air conditioning. He got a good look at Rachel. She had her hair in a bun and wore thick glasses. Otherwise she was easy on the eyes. Flat stomach. Round hips. Nice smell too. That perfume she had on made you wish she'd used more of it.

He almost didn't notice her two kids, a boy and a girl. They were sitting in the back seat, not saying a word. Well, that figured. Parents couldn't hit or yell at their kids any more. No real discipline. Yet those two weren't cutting up or fighting. Not pushing the envelope one bit. Alex wondered if they'd been getting child sized pop-Zaps or a full dose like the one he'd just taken.

"I really appreciate this," Alex said as she turned onto their street. He was proud of how he'd worked out a plan so quick under the circumstances. When they got to his house, he'd get Rachel to ring the doorbell and talk to Lisa while he watched the kids. *How the hell am I supposed to do that?* Didn't matter, he had to try. If he didn't make it back inside, he'd at least try to start his van again.

LEAVE THIS STREET.

"Rachel! Stop the truck," Alex said.

"Oh ... My ...God ... I should've known."

LEAVE NOW.

"Slow down. I've gotta get out."

"Seriously. You got on their bad side, and you're involving me."

"Well, if you'd stop the damn truck ..." Alex struggled to keep his voice calm. Last thing he needed was Rachel feeling threatened on top of everything else. They picked up on that shit.

She was still yammering. "You are not a nice person."

And she didn't have the ability to bitch him out and think about her driving at the same time. So she just kept going further up the street that Alex wasn't supposed to be on.

He opened his door and jumped. Rachel had been driving fairly slow, about ten miles-per-hour—still fast enough to make landing on his feet a challenge. Plus, Alex still wasn't right from that earlier pop-Zap.

The second his feet hit the pavement, he went sprawling and skidding into a heap. It was one of those spills where you felt the pain and didn't want to look.

Alex shifted to a sitting position. His right elbow was bleeding. And his pant leg on that side was ripped, which meant the skin underneath it hadn't done too well either. The good news was: everything moved. No broken bones. And no more booming voices in his head.

Because they were done warning him.

In a split second, they'd roughed up his insides—from the top of his head to the seat of his crotch, then all the way down to his toes—with scalding hot sandpaper. Alex screamed louder than he'd ever screamed in his life. But it was like being in an invisible bubble, cut off from the rest of the world. Nobody heard him. His yells didn't make the slightest ripple in that quiet, peaceful neighborhood. He caught a glimpse of Rachel's garage door closing. She was going on with life, oblivious to his agony.

He got back on his feet, though. Running, staggering, whatever it took to get the hell out of here ... knowing without a doubt that he wouldn't be coming back.

ALEX WAS dizzy and dripping sweat with no place to go. His pockets were empty, except for his wallet. That was something; at least he had some cash on him. He could walk to a convenience store and use their phone. *What phone, dumb-ass?* Hell, he'd forgotten. No more internet, no phone service of any kind, no TV or radio. People had to talk face-to-face or through snail-mailed letters.

All of that, and lights and appliances still worked. Go figure! A fiber-optic cable was now a useless string of crap, but copper wires still conducted electrical current just fine. That meant your flat screen TV wasn't a total loss. You could still play DVDs and games. But there was no TV signal to be had. Same thing with your stereo. CDs and tapes, no problem, but forget radio.

All of those changes had come with the shuffling—that day when everyone—not just the heavy partiers, but everyone—fell asleep and woke up somewhere different.

He stuck out his thumb every time a car approached. People hitchhiked a lot these days. They did a whole slew of things they never used to do.

A gleaming black car stopped to pick him up. Alex opened the rear passenger door and breathed in the crisp newness of the vehicle. That new car smell ... there was something that never changed. The back seat had a plastic cover over it—to protect the leather upholstery from people like him, he guessed. Whatever. He was glad to get off his feet.

The driver was a middle-aged man in an iron-colored suit that looked expensive. The girl with him had her hair tied up in a lopsided pattern that was supposed to be cool. She wore a yellow sundress with a plunging neckline. And those pearls around her neck were the size of grapes.

"Where are you going?" the man asked.

Alex opened his mouth to answer and realized he had no idea. What the hell ... might as well be honest. "To tell you the truth, I don't know," he said. "I just got ousted."

The girl smiled sympathetically. "You poor thing. We guessed that when the moment we saw you. I'm Janice. And this is my husband, Jameson."

"Janice and Jameson," Alex said. "They sure did their homework when they put the two of you together."

"Actually ..." Janice stifled a little girl's giggle. "You see ..."

"Both of us had significant others who got ousted," Jameson said.

"You're being too nice," Janice chirped. "They behaved like fools, so our wonderful *benefactors* took care of them for us."

"They take care of everything," Jameson crowed. "I mean, all the politicians ever did was talk, while our ideals and values kept slipping. I don't understand people who call them invaders. That's wrong-headed. They didn't set us back, they set us right. No more domestic violence. No more crime—well, no unpunished crime."

Alex clenched his fists. Felt his fingernails digging into his palms. Then he closed his eyes and took a couple of relaxed breaths. He had to ask. "Does it ever bother you that someone or something might be watching you all the time?"

"That's never a problem if you have nothing to hide," Jameson shot back.

Yeah, right. You're scared shitless. That's why they'd stopped to pick him up in the first place. To score brownie points with mankind's new rulers. *Look at us. We're helping the less fortunate.*

Alex decided to needle him some more. "I mean watching you *all* the time, as in 100 percent. How about when you're in bed together—or taking a crap?"

"Oooh gross!" Janice said.

Jameson's knuckles turned white from his grip on the steering wheel. "There's a crossroads coming up," he said. "We're going to have to drop you off there."

THERE WERE ALREADY four other people at the crossroads looking for rides. A car stopped and picked up three of them as Alex was getting out of Jameson's car. That left him and a skinny black kid.

At least the sun was setting; that was something. But Alex ignored the soft explosion of color in the sky that spanned the horizon with infinite width and depth. He saw only the coolness of the lengthening shadows. That was all he cared about. That heat rippling off the blacktop getting snuffed out.

Alex walked up to the kid. "You got a name?"

"Marcus." The boy stared off into the distance, avoiding eye contact.

"I'm Alex. You get ousted too?"

The boy bared a mouthful of yellow teeth. "Look mister. Take a walk. Ok?"

It was getting darker. A car's headlights washed over

them as it zoomed past, illuminating the boy's white under-shirt. "Yeah," Alex said. "I've gotta find a way to make it back too."

"Make it back?" Marcus barked a harsh laugh. "What do you mean, make it back? There ain't no going back once they oust you."

"If I can get her to—"

"Get her to do what? Tell those fuckers it's all good now. That everything's cool." His voice rose to a mocking falsetto. *"Please Mr. Alien, I ain't scared no more; you can let my baby back in now.* It don't work that way. When you're out, you're out."

Alex wanted to puke. The blood was singing in her ears. He touched the side of his face, felt the moist skin under his fingertips ... needed to know it was still there. He stared at the boy, wanting to wring his neck and to run away screaming at the same time. "What the hell do you know about it?" he demanded.

"My daddy got ousted," Marcus said. "I begged them. Told them it was my fault. Said I wasn't scared of him. But they stung him every time he tried to get near us. He still works. Pays the bills. Keeps us up as best he can, even if he can't live with us no more."

"So who are you with now?" Alex asked. He had no idea why he cared. Hell, he had enough problems of his own.

"Me and my baby sister. We never did find Momma and my two brothers; they got put somewhere else in that damn shuffling."

"I was with someone till this afternoon," Alex said. "A gal named Lisa. Former fashion model, according to her. I guess that's true. Not like I can look her up online now. Fifteen years older than me, but still holding onto her looks, at least some of them. I was pretty much alone before that ... Anyhow, she'll get foreclosed on pretty soon, unless she finds herself a sugar daddy. Then it'll be her turn to get ousted."

"Write her a letter, man. Get her to drop off some of your shit somewhere. Better than nothing."

"Waste of time," Alex said.

"You never know," Marcus replied. "Me and daddy still talk through the mail. He needed the car for work, so he mailed me a letter telling me a time and place. I parked it where he told me and left the keys. Not like anybody was going to steal it and risk getting lit up."

"Whoa. Hold on a second. They let your daddy take a car you'd parked somewhere? Just let him drive off with it?"

"Hell yeah. It's *his* car, ain't it?"

ALEX SAT ten yards from the road propped up against an oak tree. He couldn't move. His throat screamed for water. He was all alone with the smell of his own sweat and the thundering waves of pain in his head.

And nothing to do but wait. He wanted to look at his watch to see how long Marcus had been gone, but digging his hands into the leaves and the dirt underneath him anchored him somehow. It was dusk, but that didn't matter; he kept his head down, seeing only the dark outline of his splayed legs.

They'd kept trying to hitch a ride, but nobody had stopped for them. Somewhere along the way, Alex couldn't make it any further. Maybe he'd let himself get dehydrated or those pop-Zaps took something out of him. Or his body just flipped him the middle finger and shut itself down.

At any rate, Marcus had continued on to Alex's house—at least that's what he'd said he was going to do. Maybe he'd turned around and gone home. Or he could've made it there and found the van already gone. Lisa or one of the neighbors might have had it towed away. Those alien bastards could have pop-Zapped his skinny body the second he touched the door. Alex had given Marcus permission to drive his van. Said it out loud for *them* to hear. That ought to mean that Marcus wasn't stealing. But hell, this was all just guesswork ...

Alex gritted his teeth against fresh waves of pain; these were strong whirlpools of hurt eroding the back of his face. Another thought: Marcus could just take the van and there wasn't a damn thing Alex could do about it.

He closed his eyes, drifted ... and woke up gagging on warm liquid. He shifted to his knees and dry-heaved. "C'mon man. Drink some more." He recognized the voice. Marcus was standing over him, shoving a jug of water in his face.

Alex pushed the jug away. "You get it?" he croaked, his throat feeling like sandpaper.

"Yeah, man. The engine was flooded, sure enough. I pressed the gas pedal for a couple of seconds like you told me."

"Lisa?"

"I dunno. Somebody was in the house. Light came on. Face at the window." He shoved the water at Alex again. "C'mon, man. Small sips. You've gotta do this."

THE VAN RATTLED and backfired as Marcus cruised through the all-brick subdivision. Alex sat in the passenger seat, surveying the neighborhood with a pair of binoculars. Watching for signs. There were some obvious things to look for: someone frozen like a statue, or hurrying like there was no tomorrow. But there was more to it than that. Ousted people had a wild, hunted look in their eyes; you could sometimes smell their fear before you saw them. These were things that someone who'd never been ousted wouldn't know about.

At any rate, Alex and Marcus would pick them up, drive them to a safe place, and help them get back some of what they already owned ... for a cut. They'd rescued three ousted people during the past ten days: a man who'd busted a dining room chair; a woman who'd thrown a wine bottle at her husband; and a little girl who'd bit her new post-shuffle mom. The girl had nothing to offer. But Marcus had scooped her up anyhow. Another mouth to feed at his house now. And they were supposed to be doing this to get ahead ...

But ousted rescue wasn't their only business venture. Ousted people often left damaged houses behind. And Alex just happened to be a handyman. Not only that: it was easy to spot the fancy homes that looked run down—if you knew what to look for—even when there was nothing obvious on the surface. Say their car hadn't moved in a few days or the grass was overgrown. Any signs of neglect meant things weren't going good. And folks had to spruce up the property to sell it off.

No luck so far this morning, and they'd finished cruising this neighborhood. So they did what they always did: stopped for lunch and got ready to move on to the next development.

"My baby sister's getting brainwashed at school," Marcus remarked. "Teachers are calling these assholes *benefactors* now. Saying they're stimulating human evolution. Mixing things up, redistributing all wealth. Seeing who gets to rise to the top. All that, while stopping us from hurting each other."

Alex threw his cigarette out the window. "Know what I think: they're fucking with us. Because they get off on that shit."

Marcus stared out the window. "There's gotta be a way to kill those bastards," he said.

"They can hear us talking," Alex said. "You know that, don't you?"

"What do they care? Not like they've got anything to worry about from us. We're just adapting to all this new shit."

"Yeah, well, let's adapt our way into some money today. I've got a repair job to go to if we don't spot an ousted person pretty soon."

Marcus was right, though. About them not being a threat. Or was he? Sure, they were adapting to the situation as best they could. But their business model was a loophole in this unseen and unspoken alien rule. Maybe even a tiny crack.

Here they were: two people who never would've had much to do with one another ... having to work together. Trust each other.

Right now, it seemed like the only way to get at those bastards.

VIRAL

Once upon a time, there were running shoe brands like Nike, Saucony, Brooks, Mizuno. Different looks, and also different feels based on size, foot type, and running style. Some brands were lightweight, others offered stability; some promised a softer ride.

But the thing with antigravity shoes ... well, they were a marketing nightmare. A real bitch.

That's where Thomas came in.

His challenge with this particular product: running with anti-gravs felt about the same for everyone. Whether you weighed eighty or two hundred pounds. Didn't matter. It was a floaty sensation of your feet touching the ground just enough to give you traction. And industry standards being so freaking strict—especially when it came to enabling people to do things beyond their normal physical capabilities—made one brand name pretty much the same as another.

The sun had just set on a clear Thursday evening in November. Thomas never noticed. He sat alone at his desk, literally walled in by floating holograms of graphs and spreadsheets.

And somewhere amid these mountains of data was *that* critical piece of info, which would provide a surefire way to pinpoint *that* target market.

Bullshit! He only kept the holos up for show. And to give himself some semblance of privacy in the wide-open work environment his company insisted on. *Can't get cubicle walls, use holograms.*

Besides, finding *that* market was total bunk. True marketing meant VIRAL. Impressed—no, imprinted!—into public opinion. Appealing to eighteen-year-old girls, middle-aged married men, young headbangers in their twenties. Everybody with access to the net. How's that for a target?

His normal approach was to put on the noise-cancelling headphones and pretend to study the floating stats around him. In reality, he was cleaning the muck out of his mind and waiting for an idea to strike him.

The idea would come. It always did. It was inevitable.

But Thomas was stuck at the moment.

Clear your mind. First thing that pops in your head. Go with that.

No use. His creative fire had been doused by a nagging sense of dread. Not a *this is going to be a pain in the ass* kind of dread. No. This dread was more of the *I'm shitting bricks* variety.

Thomas took a deep breath. It was definitely time to stop these bullshit mind games he was playing with himself.

Yeah. Jack had been fired. Because Thomas had baited him into saying the wrong thing when he thought his audio was muted. (Wonder how it got unmuted!)

So what? Jack's own mouth had stamped his ticket to

unemployment. He never could shut up and play along. Besides, Thomas needed support, not competition. He certainly didn't need someone trying to one-up him in the conference room.

Thing is, Jack's threats as they were walking him out the door ... amounted to nothing. *Pay us all back! Good luck with that, Bub.*

Now, twenty years ago, a guy like Jack would have been downright scary. A prime candidate to show up at his former place of employment with a gun. But not today. The scanners would detect any unauthorized weapon—be it modern zapper or traditional firearm. Perimeter bots would surround an intruder before he could blink.

Dammit all! He'd removed a creative obstacle without getting caught. No imminent danger. No threat of any kind. All clear sailing from here. And yet, he still had nothing in the way of ideas.

Hey, lighten up. Thomas chided himself one last time. *Something will pop in your brain. It always does. This isn't life or death.*

What he failed to notice was the silent drone hovering over his head.

THEY PINGED HIM AGAIN. It was time for the late evening team summit—code for *collaboration with morons.*

Thomas sighed. Selling them on a killer concept he'd dreamed up was always an uphill battle. Going in there with nothing was really going to suck.

Worse still: there was no tingle this time. The reason he'd chosen this career in the first place. The electric charge of his imaginings becoming realities. Realities that shaped and influenced mass audiences worldwide.

Like propagating part of himself around the whole planet! People eating, sleeping, breathing his concept. Controlled by him. Hell, his sphere of influence might someday encompass the entire freaking universe. How cool was that?

Another ping. Third reminder. This one from his manager.

Thomas slapped his desk in frustration; he never even considered looking up. Thus, the drone remained unnoticed.

BEFORE HEADING to the conference room, Thomas got out his sample pair of anti-gravs. They were plain brown loafers. A huge problem right there. There was nothing to work with. No flashy colors or bright laces. They looked more like a cross between slippers and dress shoes than high-octane performance apparel. Which eliminated a lot of the obvious tag lines. Couldn't use *Some Like it Hot* for hushpuppies. And *death defying, hell raising,* and *kickass* were also out.

Still, Thomas slipped them on, feeling them hug his feet. Snug, but not too tight. Yeah, great fit. Comfortable ride. But nothing special. At any rate, he might as well take advantage of the indistinguishable product he was saddled with promoting. He could at least say he'd been walking around in them, looking for inspiration.

He glided over to the conference room and paused at the door. There was an overhead screen on the far wall; a long table ate up most of the floor space. And they could see him standing there. Sure, they could. The walls were clear glass (to promote open communication). A dozen people in a room large enough for eight.

What do you do? You bull you way forward.

Thomas burst in talking. "Hey guys! I've been crunching the numbers and found some interesting patterns." A crock, but what did they know?

Nothing registered on any faces. They were all staring—no, gaping! Distracted by something. Hell, they weren't looking at him at all …

"Hi, Thomas."

Shit! Jack's voice. Coming from above.

Thomas looked up and immediately recognized the drone. How could he not? This was a manufacturer sample of another product they'd recently pitched. It hovered about four feet overhead, just below the white ceiling tiles.

Freebird. Catchy name for a drone with a crazy long flight time. Jack had come up with that one.

"Okay. Everybody check out the wall screen," Jack's drone voice instructed. "Hey! Everybody! Look at the damn wall screen now."

Heads turned obediently. Then dead silence. The air went out of the room. They were watching themselves onscreen from an overhead camera angle. Clearly, the drone was filming them and streaming the video.

Thomas spotted himself. His blockish body looked sleeker than it was in the custom-fitted slacks and shirt he was wearing. Thomas also noted that he was the only one in the room who looked composed at all; everyone else was gawking in stunned silence. As if they were looking in a carnival mirror and didn't recognize their own reflections. Or maybe they were shocked by their helpless appearance.

A couple of youngish guys slid along the back wall, working their way toward the door. Idiots! Like Jack wouldn't see them plain as day.

Sure enough. "Touch that door and everyone in this room dies," Jack said.

"What are you going to do?" one of the guys asked. He was tall with spiked hair and the face of a falcon. "I'll bust that drone into tiny pieces."

He had a point. A plastic drone could ram into you. Those propellers would probably hurt. But you could still win that battle if you had the balls to risk losing a finger. For now, though, the drone was simply hovering out of reach.

"Do me a favor," Jack said. "Take a picture of the drone's undercarriage."

Several people hurried to comply.

"Okay. Now project it onscreen."

"Good. Now go to the *United Global* website. Search for terrorism. Now weapons. Good. Now drill down into plastic explosives. Click on K10. Right there. Compare their photo with the picture you just took. Notice any similarities?"

The would-be escapees looked crestfallen. A couple of women started to cry.

Wrapped in the telltale black packaging, a K10 cylinder (the size and shape of a long Tootsie Roll), was attached to the bottom of the drone.

"Feel free to read up on the specifics," Jack said. "There's enough firepower to blow this office to smithereens. All I've got to do is press the magic button."

IT DIDN'T TAKE LONG. One of the women, a mom in her early thirties, made her plea. "I've got two young children at home." Her tears were real.

As was Jack's callousness. "None of this is on me," he said. "I'm just reacting to an unfortunate situation. So clam up, or I'll nuke the whole room."

The woman choked back sobs. A couple of coworkers moved closer to her; one of them held her hand. Pockets of people started whispering among themselves. The team's manager, a portly man in his fifties, was hugging himself and muttering—a quivering blob of uselessness.

Thomas cursed inwardly. *Christ Almighty,* he thought. *Jammed into this glass cage like sardines with this asshole holding us hostage. How?* It made no sense. Building security ought to be able to put Jack out of business simply by jamming the drone's radio frequency.

Yep. That's how drones worked. Thomas knew. Part of pitching a product entailed a rudimentary understanding of its functionality. A drone used a unique identification code to identify a transmission on one particular radio frequency as the transmission it wanted to receive.

Jack would know that too. He'd been point person on the campaign. Until he wasn't.

At any rate, he'd somehow highjacked the demo device. They'd disabled all of his accounts, taken his access badge; two armed guards had escorted him out of the building. Standard protocol when someone got canned. He wasn't getting back in. But nobody had thought to check any of the sample products that he might have gotten his hands on. Duh!

"And now! The moment you've all been waiting for!" Jack's proclamation startled the room into a collective flinch.

Onscreen, a chat window had opened. A girl was on camera. A striking girl in her twenties.

Amanda! She and Thomas had been an item. Except that they were taking a break—as she put it. A really long break, but what the hell.

"So tell us how you know Thomas," Jack said.

Amanda's pretty face wrinkled for a moment before she answered. "We dated for a while."

"Hey, Jack. How about leaving her out of this?" Thomas said.

"She's signed into this party under her own volition," Jack said. "Nobody's forcing her. I'm not in her physical vicinity. Nowhere near. She can log off and get on with her life anytime she's ready."

Thomas clenched his teeth and looked down at his phone. *Get on with her life.* Bile scourged the back of his throat on that one. He thought about texting Amanda. Something lame like *What's up?* Right. They could both see firsthand what was up.

That's when it hit him.

Drones used WiFi for offloading video footage and firmware updates. Never for navigation. Well, almost never. It was actually possible, just pointless in most cases. You'd be limited to a very small area. But in this case, where a drone only needed to navigate the confines of a single floor in an office ... It could hook into the building's WiFi and allow Jack to control it from there.

Meanwhile, Jack was still talking. "I did make her aware that logging out before I give the okay would cause an explosion in a certain office. Here's a question: is she cooperating to help Thomas or the other slobs in the room with him?

"Yo! Amanda! That was a question for *you.*"

Amanda didn't flinch. "None of these people deserve to get hurt," she said.

"None, really? You know that for a fact?"

"You know it too," Amanda said.

"Whoa. Words of wisdom from the ... is it receptionist or cocktail waitress this week?"

"Better than unemployed loser," Thomas said.

"Now I see the attraction," Jack said. "He considers your career path a cut above *unemployed* or *loser*. See? He respects you for who you are. And I'll bet you thought it was purely sexual."

Thomas hoped that Jack would think he was avoiding eye contact. When, in fact, he was texting furiously under the table. He wasn't friendly with any of his coworkers outside of the office. But he had the personal contact info of everyone in the company. Scott Hogan was head of the I.T. department. He was the guy who kept their network humming. And just the man for the task that Thomas had in mind.

He fired off his text, knowing he'd botched some words in the process. *Shut down our interconnecti. Jack is controllng the drne thru WaFi.*

Then somebody shook him—too hard to just be getting his attention. He could feel panic in those hands gripping his shoulders.

"We're going to play a game," Jack said. "It's called kick the shit out of Thomas."

Everyone shifted nervously. A collective twitch fluttered across everyone in the confined space.

"The rules are simple," Jack said. "There's only one. You beat Thomas to a pulp. Right here and now. On live feed. With his girlfriend watching. Oh, and Amanda, you're going to cheer them on. I should make you change into a cheerleader outfit, but I'll be nice."

Nobody moved.

Thomas felt his crotch turn to water; he wanted to puke. But you didn't show fear to a deranged guy like Jack. You didn't dare show fear. "What happens if I fight my way out of this room?" he asked.

"I blow it up," Jack said. "Hear that, folks? You let this worm slither out of here and you're toast."

The two young assertive guys slid over to block the door. A couple of others stood up.

"C'mon. What are you waiting for?"

"Wait a minute!" Thomas yelled. "At least let the women go." That sounded good. It would buy more time. And maybe give him a chance to break for the door.

"Sorry," Jack said. "But I'm afraid we're all in this together. Tell you what—I'll give a countdown. That'll give you a chance to prepare yourself. You can try to run or hide. Or beg. That'd be good. Oh, and guys, if you're not stomping him through the floor when I get to zero ...

Anyhow, here goes: ten, nine, eight ..."

The phone vibrated in Thomas' hand. Scott's reply text said: *Can't risk taking down the network. Jack's already messaged us. Says bomb will explode if internet connection is broken.*

WAIT! Thomas willed his spinning brain to slow down.

Okay. Say Jack planned this out in advance ... suppose —just suppose—he'd wanted to arm the drone with a K10 explosive pack while he still worked here. Could he do it?

No. Hell no. They'd detect bomb residue the moment he set foot on the grounds. He'd never get in in the building. Making this whole situation one ginormous bluff.

Probably.

Jack's voice got louder. "Five, four ..."

"Is this worth it to you?" Amanda asked.

"Go far so good," Jack replied.

"Why? I mean, what are you getting out of this? What's the payoff?"

"Oh my. Someone's been reading the self-help section in the magazine aisle."

"Fine, Jack. Whatever. I don't have a fancy diploma. Guys like you and Thomas leave me in the dust with your big vocabulary. But I can face myself in the mirror and know I'm a good person."

She has a good heart, Thomas thought to himself. Couldn't think her way out of a wet paper bag. But you felt safe around her. He could almost smell the newness of her leather jacket and that herbal shampoo she used.

Meanwhile, Jack had gone totally silent. Amanda had distracted him. She'd hit a nerve. More importantly, she'd stopped the countdown. She was like that. Things always seemed to work out for her.

And for him at the moment. But what to do? Jack could play this game all day. The authorities weren't about to risk it.

Thomas feverishly shot out another text: *Have bots scan room for explosives. He's bluffing.*

Nobody moved. The room had become a still image. Thomas got to his feet and grabbed the table just in time. How had he forgotten about the anti-gravs he was wearing?

"You bitch," Jack said to Amanda. "You clueless bitch.

You have no idea about Thomas. No clue what he did behind your back. Actually, *you* tell her."

"Me?" Thomas said.

"Yeah, you. Asshole. Right here, right now. The whole world's watching. Let's talk about that conference in Vegas last summer. And don't you dare lie."

Thomas looked down at the carpet and said nothing.

The drone moved closer, stopping right above him. "C'mon," Jack said. "No sense in getting everybody blown up. Even though we both know you'd let it happen if you thought it would advance your career."

Thomas watched Amanda wipe away a tear. She seemed to be looking straight at him, although it was hard to be sure of that; after all, she was watching the entire room on her viewing screen; plus, she was listening to Jack's ranting. Still he had to look away.

"Hey!" Someone shoved him. "Start talking."

"Better listen to him," Jack said.

Thomas glanced down at his phone. No response to his last text. Bunch of chickenshits! Too scared of being wrong to act. Like as not, there was no way—absolutely no way—for Jack to smuggle in explosive material. On the other hand, absolute certainty was impossible ...

Screw it.

Thomas leaped.

Jack obviously wasn't expecting that because the drone made no evasive move whatsoever. It was easy. Thomas was able to grab the drone with both hands, while keeping his fingers away from the props. No problem at all. Then, on his descent, he slammed it down on the table. Hard. The drone's plastic hull shattered with a satisfying crack.

Several women screamed. A couple of guys dove under

the table. The room was in a collective panic. You could feel the electricity from it all. Pure fear-driven panic.

Thomas grinned till he thought his face would split. No explosion. No loud kaboom. No flying shrapnel. Nothing. Nada. Jack had been bluffing all along.

He'd been right. You couldn't sneak explosives into a secure building. What the hell was everyone thinking? All of them—getting played like a symphony of cheap violins. Made to dance like puppets on strings. Or fill in whatever other diminutive metaphors you wanted for a bunch of prize boobs.

Thomas leaped onto the table. "Conference room cameras on!" he yelled. The wall screen, which had gone blank when he'd downed the drone, came to life. Amanda's image was gone. Connection broken. They were now filming themselves in the room and streaming the video out to the world.

"Thomas! What the hell are you doing?" Abigail Peters asked.

"Strap in and enjoy the ride," Thomas said. "We're about to go VIRAL."

The protests came from all sides. *Are you nuts? What the hell is wrong with you?*

Thomas shouted over them. "Watch and learn! This is a dream come true." His blood was racing; the creative fire roared in his belly. His spirit was reignited. He was a flame eater, a sword swallower. A different breed. Nothing like those ordinary rank and file rubes who went about their day with no concept of what was happening to them at any given moment. He, Thomas, was a fine-tuned genius.

And standing above them on the table, he felt only disdain. Yeah, disdain for the dimwits he had to carry along with him on a daily basis. Just look at them. Gawking.

Mouths hanging open in disbelief. No comprehension of the opportunity that had just fallen into their laps.

Thomas started shouting. More from enthusiasm than frustration. "Zoom in on my feet. The shoes. You know ... the product line we're here to promote. Think about it. Regular guy in loafers saves the day. How's this for a slogan: *you don't have to be an action figure to be a badass.*

"And why are you all looking at me like I've got three heads? I mean, c'mon. Crisis averted. We've got a golden opportunity here. Let's roll with it."

The two young, assertive types headed for the door, as did several other people. Everyone else stared at Thomas in stunned silence.

Thomas ignored them. "How about this. Somebody pull up that old song, *Secret Agent Man.* We have those lyrics going while a regular guy walks into the office wearing anti gravs. Then have him do something insanely cool. Hell, every commercial could be a new adventure ...

"Guys? Hey! Work with me here."

BOOM!

IT HAPPENED RIGHT under his feet. The bomb went off and his anti gravs reacted.

Thomas shot straight up and almost hit the ceiling. The only thing he felt on his way down was sick terror.

His feet touching down on the table came as a shock. He staggered for a moment, then regained his footing. The table was still solid and intact. As were his feet and legs.

Oh, shit!

Everywhere he looked. All over the room. Red splattered on the walls. People moaning and bleeding.

The young assertive had his legs blown off. No. He was on his knees, dripping red and puking his guts out. Pretty much intact physically. In fact, nobody looked dead. Some were crying softly, others cursing profusely. A few were pacing around like trapped rodents. Everybody seemed to have survived. With the exception of their manager, who was slumped down on his back in a corner. He didn't look well at all.

Thomas felt a warmth spreading down his thighs. Looking down, he realized that he'd wet his pants. And he was draped in red like everyone else, mostly from the waist down.

The sight of the room, of the people in it, and his own condition make him dizzy. He sat down hard on the tabletop, right next to the battered drone.

Hey. Just a goddamned minute!

The drone should have been blown to oblivion. And the glass walls ought to be shattered. And everybody was still alive. Thomas felt of his leg. He rolled up his pants. Not so much as a blemish. No actual blood. This was some sort of red dye.

And that explosion, come to think of it ... more shock than substance. A sudden boom, sure, but not the eardrum buster you'd expect.

It all made sense. Jack hadn't smuggled in explosive material (back to the bots detecting that). His bomb wasn't explosive at all. Just a red dye pack that ruptured when heated up. The seal could be broken with a pinprick. Not terribly hard to rig. Add to that the fact that Jack had accompanied his 'explosion' with a loud boom over the audio system.

All an elaborate hoax ... and for what?

ONE WEEK LATER ...

Thomas looked at his phone. Again. For about the eightieth time today. Still no response from Amanda. And why not? He'd only texted her a dozen times since the incident—explaining, rationalizing, apologizing, even groveling.

Still, staring at the empty message queue on his phone beat the hell out of looking at his surroundings. He was in the unemployment office waiting area. Way overdressed for this shit! He was sitting in a rickety chair that you couldn't give away at a yard sale. And the thought of his silk suit touching it made him cringe. But he'd been forced to sit rather than stand. Yeah, the wait was that long.

Looking around the room was flat depressing. A hard luck crowd. Life had kicked them in the ass and they weren't getting up anytime soon. Some of them knew it. You could tell by their unshaven faces and rumpled clothes that they'd given up. Unable to compete in normal society. So screw it. Might as well suck on the government tit for as long as they could. Others were bright and hopeful. A couple of the boys in their late teens were wearing ties; a heavyset girl was in a skirt that could double as a throw rug. They were in for a rude awakening. Nobody with prospects frequented this dump.

Thomas closed his eyes and tried to remind himself that he was sitting here, breathing in the stale air of resignation, only as a stopgap. A way to defray expenses until he found another job.

About that new job ... he was toxic at the moment. Damaged goods. All because he'd gotten his wish. The footage had gone VIRAL. That part with him standing on the table disparaging his coworkers might not have been so bad ...

Until the explosion.

Tens of millions of views and counting. And the comments ... didn't even want to think about reading those.

"Number fifty-two."

Thomas stood. His turn. He had a paper tag with his number in line, like the kind you get at a butcher's shop. Which made sense. This place dealt in dead meat.

They directed him to sit in another dingy chair next to a utilitarian desk. The man behind the desk had a yellowed white shirt and a greasy combover. Round and hunched. A bureaucrat who would gladly monitor peeling paint as part of his job and never get bored. He could be forty or sixty. Didn't matter. His life wasn't going to change over time. Neither was he.

"Name?"

"Thomas Miller."

The man's nameplate identified him as Hershel Wiggins. Thomas surveyed the desk and noticed photos of Hershel and his family—a plain woman with thick glasses and two teenage kids. There was a photo of a camper parked at a public campground. Classy.

Hershel Wiggins hit the keys on his keyboard one laborious stroke at a time. Then he looked up from his computer screen and locked his gaze onto Thomas. Recognition flared in his eyes. Recognition and disdain. His voice was smug, his smile cold as hell. "I'm sorry, Mr. Miller, but you fail to qualify for benefits."

"You're kidding," Thomas said.

Hershel ignored him. "I've just sent a copy of the denial to your phone," he said.

"But I didn't quit. My employer—"

"Terminated your employment with just cause."

"No. Bullshit. I was an exemplary employee."

"We're done here. Have a nice day."

"Wait. You can't just kick me out." Thomas felt his scalp prickle. "I've got rights."

"Time's up, Mr. Miller. I need to move on to the next in line."

"I'm not leaving."

THOMAS SAT on a cold park bench, eyes tearing from the harsh sun and bitter wind. He'd just read the claim denial for the fifth time.

It was all there—what his company had to say about him. Thomas had talent. He could sell his ass off. A top producer. They deeply regretted having to lose him as an employee. As such, they were *NOT* contesting his unemployment claim. Wishing him only the best of luck in his future endeavors.

The denial?

The unemployment agency had made that call on their own. More specifically, Hershel *Fuck Head* Wiggins had made a discretionary decision. Didn't happen often, but in this case, in light of aggravating circumstances ... the esteemed Mr. F.H. Wiggins had even included a link to the video.

Thomas started a new text to Amanda, then deleted it. What the hell could he say? *I'm freezing my ass off on a park bench with nothing to do and nowhere to go. Please feel sorry for me.* Yeah, all alone. Even the pigeons had pegged him as a loser. They never even paused to see if he'd scatter some crumbs.

Okay. Enough already. A single incident didn't define who you were. It might take a few months, but eventually, this shit storm would die down.

Right. Thomas blew his nose and wiped his eyes again.

That's not how VIRAL worked.

RAY GUN REVIVAL

When Jeb Pruitt's wife couldn't forgive him, he kept his weapons collection and gave her everything else.

He started selling a few pieces of his collection online and at local shows, the bartering and swapping providing a welcome distraction from his life. Before long, a weekend booth morphed into a brick-and-mortar shop that dealt in anything from the 17th century longsword to the modern-day eliminator.

Now those were two different weapons for you. The longsword was five pounds of double-edged steel, while the eliminator rested in the palm of your hand and waited for you to press the *Remove* button. And yet, they shared a common objective: it was all about separating atoms. Granted, the brute force of hacking through flesh and bone represented a huge departure from push-button dissemination. But, either way, you were doing bad things to your adversary's molecular structure.

Jeb was sitting behind the counter, eating his lunch from the hash house up the block. While he'd seen huge technological advances during his life, greasy fries hadn't changed in over a hundred years, according to the search engines. So Jeb had armed himself with a plastic ketchup bottle. Enough of that, and you could eat cardboard.

He stared at the countertop and his reflection stared back at him. This was a wood counter that broke every fire code in the book. It was just that synthetic paneling seemed dead next to the warm reddish-brown hue of real cherry. Jeb also didn't believe in sprinkler systems. A dousing of water or halon could be a hell of a lot harder on his merchandise than a little fire and smoke. So he kept an extinguisher on the wall behind the counter. Next to the safe.

THE BURGER TURNED to sand in his mouth when the two men walked through the door. He could almost smell something wrong about them. The first man was tall and lean with chin whiskers and a black ponytail, his bare arms tattooed past the point of saturation. His right hand gripped a plastic briefcase. His companion was the size of a barn with wide eyes and a nervous grin. Jeb's gut clenched. This boy was no more than twenty. Same age Andy would have been ...

"You'll need to leave your weapons in that box by the door," Jeb said.

"Thought this was a weapons shop," the big one drawled.

Jeb touched the eliminator on his hip. "I ain't asking," he said. "Stick 'em in the box or get out." He watched as the two men unclipped phase shifters from their holsters and laid them in the lockbox. When the lock indicator flashed acknowledgement, he locked eyes with the lean one.

"Alright, let's see what you've got in that case. And it better not be armed, whatever it is."

As shady as these guys were, Jeb welcomed their intrusion. All during lunch, he'd been wrestling with his thoughts—well, fantasies—about Linda. Normal, healthy aspirations, really. Both of their bodies were sound thanks to vitalization therapy, which entailed outright organ replacement and musculoskeletal rejuvenation. So with old-age frailty eliminated, they could engage in all sorts of youthful activities with no worry about broken hips or cardiac failure. One downside, however: it was a lot like putting a new engine in an old car and skipping the paint job. And plastic surgery looked downright scary after age eighty.

Linda didn't go in for that cosmetic crap. Didn't need to. It wasn't like she was hurting in the looks department. Sure, her skin was lined, but what of it? She had the green eyes of a schoolgirl. More important: when they'd sit and talk, the hours would melt away to nothing.

Thing is, Jeb couldn't bring himself to do anything about it. Not after what had happened with Andy. He'd told Linda all about that, but her saying it wasn't his fault made no difference.

Some threats couldn't be eliminated. No way to zap away remorse. And even if you could, who's to say you wouldn't wreck things all over again.

When the lean man set the case on the counter and flipped it open, Jeb's heart pounded like a jackhammer. But his face remained placid—nary a twitch in his bushy eyebrows as he stared down his long nose at what was perhaps the most significant find he'd ever seen.

It was a mint condition NA-One, a relic of huge innovative and historical value. This was the first hand-held particle beam weapon, and the only one to resemble the lead-shooting pistol.

And lethal! Particle beam weaponry was a triple death threat: thermal damage via the massive voltage, kinetic penetration due to subatomic particles moving at light speed, and disruption of the target's atomic bonds. No concept of a stun setting for human victims like the ones in those ancient TV shows. After all, from a survival standpoint, did it matter if an egg wound up hard or soft-boiled?

"Mind if I take it out of the case?" Jeb asked.

The man nodded approval, so Jeb examined the weapon with an expert's eye. Lightweight magnesium. Less sturdy than steel, but no recoil either. He put it under his magnifier, noting the etchings on the handle just below the squeeze bulb. "This here's a first model," he announced. "Not many of those left."

This early hand-held lacked the firepower of the tripod-mounted cannons that preceded it. So for some extra oomph, they'd integrated sodium atoms into the beam it fired. Sodium combined with water produced a fierce explosion, due to the liberated hydrogen atoms. And a human body just happened to be sixty-percent water.

"What's it worth?" the big one demanded.

"Depends on whether it can hit a target," Jeb said.

The pair looked at each other and shrugged. "Well, you can see it's in one piece," the lean one said. "Any way you could meet us somewhere between the price of a working model and a dud?"

"Not a chance," Jeb said. "Way too much difference in value for that." These boys had no clue what they had. Well, he'd give them a fair price. He wasn't in business to clip anybody. "If you're serious about it," he said, "I can charge it up right here for you. And there's a firing range out back. Everything we need to test this baby, including the robot."

"We don't need a robot," the lean man said.

"You don't understand," Jeb said. "Any man that squeezes that bulb when this model is charged—"

"Is a real man," the fat boy said. "Not some dried up old sissy."

Jeb felt his face get hot. Ten years ago, Fat Boy would have been spitting teeth. But that was before ...

"You just charge it up and fill some barrels, Grandpa," the lean man said.

Jeb touched his eliminator again. "Fill 'em yourself," he said. "Several of them. And you let the robot do the shooting."

No need trying to reason with these two. It was like arguing with children about ice cream. Thing is, this token model had a firmware flaw, which sometimes caused it to target the person firing it. Not all of the time. But it was like flipping a coin with every shot. Or playing Russian roulette.

Jeb charged up the gun, and calibrated the "robot," which was merely a clawlike gripper anchored to a swivel on a metal table. His fingers clacked across a keyboard on a sliding tray in back of the table, and a hologram plotted out tick marks for angle and distance, flashing them in midair so that the user could look straight through them at the target.

He watched as the two men muscled the last barrel of water into place. Idiots. They could have saved themselves a pair of broken backs by rolling out empty barrels and filling them with the hose. One barrel was the size of two beer kegs stacked on top of each other. Over thirty gallons of water sloshing around in there.

Barrels did make the best targets for beam firing, though. They exploded like erupting geysers.

Jeb wiped damp palms on his pant legs, then ran his fingers across the gun's smooth surface. After a final sighting check, he fitted the Na-One into the robotic claw. There wasn't much aiming entailed, this being a point-and-shoot type of weapon, but the sighting algorithm also provided feedback on beam purity and alignment. Whether or not this particular gun fell within the specifications for its class would affect its value.

The two men walked up, dripping sweat. "Ready to go," Jeb informed them. A twinge of excitement tickled his spine, despite having to deal with these lowlifes.

The lean man spat on the tile floor, then strode over the table and wrenched the NA-One out of the robotic claw.

Jeb's shout froze in his throat. What did you say to a fool who was about to jump off a rooftop or step in front of a train? Stop or I'll shoot?

All he could do was run inside before the first barrel exploded.

He almost collapsed with relief when he saw that the man was okay. "Look, I see it fires," he called out to them. "Come on inside now. I'll give you a fair price." He hated the desperation in his voice.

But he might as well have been talking to a wall. He turned away so he wouldn't have to see what was bound to come, listening to the explosions as the lean man shot the other four targets, his fat friend hooting and laughing after each one.

Five shots in all.

Even one or two was damn fool crazy. Five was a death wish.

They came in, grinning like the morons they were. Being lucky was better than being smart sometimes.

"Okay, what'll you take for her?" Jeb asked, mopping his brow.

The lean man pointed the NA-One. "Everything you've got," he said.

JEB CURSED UNDER HIS BREATH. The eliminator on his belt might as well have been a mile away. But why would he walk around with it in his hand? There were no armed weapons in the store that could hurt him—unless you counted the NA-One, which, for all intent and purpose, wasn't a viable weapon at all. Like as not, this fool would blow himself up on the next shot.

But Jeb's hand froze useless against his side. They might've stumbled onto that one good apple in a rotten barrel, in this case: a reliable weapon. Probably not, but still ... could anyone really predict the number of shots between failures?

"You touch that eliminator on your hip and I'll splatter you all over this room," the lean man said.

"Or you'll blow *yourself* up," Jeb said. "You've been lucky so far, but you're walking on a mine field. That gun in your hand ... they hadn't worked the kinks out of the scanner. Damn thing was obsolete by the time they got it right."

"Who do you think you're shitting?"

Jeb shrugged. "Your funeral," he said, reminding himself of the odds one more time.

The paper cup on the counter exploded, spraying sticky debris all over.

Jeb wiped his eyes. *Well, the damn thing nailed that half-empty cup without a hitch,* he thought. *I'd have a hell of a mess if he'd picked the ketchup bottle.* His gaze shifted to the remnants of his lunch, now scattered across the floor behind the counter. The ketchup bottle had fallen back there as well.

The tall man pointed the NA-One at Jeb again. "I'm done playing with you," he said. "You drag your white-haired self over to that safe. Now." Six shots and he was still unscathed. It was sure enough April Fool's Day in Hell.

The fat boy snickered. "Grandpa'll look like a frog in a microwave."

Neither of them was the least bit worried about anything going wrong with what amounted to an antique weapon. It was crazy as Dillinger deciding to rob a bank with a dueling pistol that hadn't been fired in decades.

Now wait a minute ... they knew something. Not the value of the gun, nor that they could have made more money just dealing straight with him, assuming the gun itself wasn't stolen, which it probably was. But they were 100-percent positive about being able to fire it with impunity.

Jeb looked at the lean man's face, at the hard, joyless expression of someone incapable of loving anyone or anything, including himself. He'd be able to kill this man. Fat Boy ... well, that was another story. Young and stupid. Probably not a bad kid, just a little off ... he shoved a memory out of his head. Maybe it wouldn't come to that.

His gaze traveled down the man's painted arms to the hand that gripped the NA-One. Fingers a bit too blockish under his black gloves. Like cubes hinged together.

Yeah ... that made sense.

Jeb was standing behind the counter; the safe was behind him and to his left. Walking over to it meant putting himself totally in the open. Of course, they'd kill him once they got whatever money he had in there. So cooperating was out.

He stepped out of his shoes and turned towards the safe in a slow and deliberate tread.

Why was he sweating over the prospect of killing the fat boy? As if in response to that question, his mind offered up a memory: Andy as a toddler, chubby legs pumping as he ran up to jump in Jeb's lap. They all said it wasn't his fault. But waking up with it every morning was something else.

"Time's up, Grandpa," the lean man said.

It sure as hell was.

Jeb stepped out into the open area, then dove behind the counter. Grabbing the nearest shoe he'd left on the floor, he slung it hard against the back wall six feet from where he lay. They couldn't see behind the counter. If they reacted to the noise ...

A surge of dirty energy raped the air, followed by the smell of toxic burn. The ketchup bottle exploded. Red everywhere. Splotches on the walls and on the ceiling. Funny ... the water content of ketchup wasn't something you'd ever consider unless your life depended on it.

The lean man had shot through the side of the counter, leaving a flaming hole—a widening ring of fire that popped and hissed in earnest. Well, of course. All real wood retained some level of moisture. With the NA-One's subatomic penetration, it was like dropping a chunk of sodium into a swimming pool.

Then Jeb heard the lean man say, without emotion: "He's toast. Let's grab what we can and clear out of here."

That was Jeb's cue. He stood and fired, and the lean man shriveled into a sizzling heap. Fat Boy didn't seem to notice. He was on his knees, puking, obviously mistaking the splattered ketchup for Jeb's blood. No stomach for this shit.

The smell of burning rubber hung in the air. Jeb hopped over the counter and confirmed his suspicions. Sure enough: there was a smoldering metallic arm and a section of leg from the same material. This man had been in some kind of accident and had a couple of robotic limbs. That explained why he could fire the NA-One without blowing himself up. No moisture in metal at all. Still, being that close to the gun during a firing cycle was beyond dumb.

Now Jed faced another problem: his counter was burning fast. His finger froze on the button that would zap Fat Boy out of existence. Something in his gut urged him to do it while he had a chance.

But the kid seemed to have shut down. He was hunched over and sniveling. *Hell, he can't do nothing,* Jeb decided. All of the store weapons were unarmed. The weapons they'd brought in with them were secured in the lockbox at the door. That made the NA-One the only dangerous weapon in the place, other than Jeb's own eliminator, and Fat Boy couldn't fire it with his flesh and blood hands, even if he did manage to grow a set of stones.

Jeb ran for the fire extinguisher. No point in getting the fire department involved. Air purifiers would eliminate the smoke. Aside from the wood counter, the rest of the shop had been coated with heat retardant plasma spray, a prudent safeguard considering the nature of Jeb's merchandise.

Not only that: he had his reasons for keeping the authorities out of this thing.

Eighteen-year-old Andy had called him from jail one time too many. With all of the jams that boy had gotten himself into, leaving him in there to learn a lesson had seemed the only sane choice. Even so, Jeb's guilt remained. Always there, chipping away in the background. It was as if he'd been the one who stabbed Andy in a fight over a soft drink.

As he extinguished the flames, Jeb worked out the details in his mind. Technically, Fat Boy could be considered a bystander. The lean man had been the one who tried to rob him.

He'd give the boy a fair price on the NA-One—hold off registering it for a while, just in case it was stolen. Give him a chance to get clear. Bottom line: offer him a fresh start instead of wasting him. This boy had just gotten an object lesson, seen how it felt to be sickened by blood and death. He just needed a chance to do things different. That's all.

But when he set down the extinguisher and turned around, the fat boy was gone. Nothing there except the steaming heap that had once been the lean man.

"Over here, Grandpa." Fat Boy's voice came from the range.

When Jeb looked, a sense of dread and disbelief made his crotch draw up into his abdomen. The boy had mounted the NA-One into the robotic claw. The hologram was down, but he could still point and shoot from the keypad.

"Lay that eliminator on the counter, real slow," he instructed.

Jeb did as he was told. This kid needed to get out of the robbery business in a hurry. Any robber with a lick of sense would have made Jeb toss his weapon across the room. As it was, the thing was still within reach. Then again, he was the one being held at gunpoint.

"Now walk over to that safe." Fat Boy's voice was just a shade too high. The stress working on him.

"You know this isn't necessary," Jeb called back.

"Get over there now!" the fat boy squealed.

"Alright, alright. Don't ..."

Oh, shit. Linda was coming down the walkway. She had her earbuds in, oblivious to the world around her. That cute little smile on her face.

"I mean it, Grandpa," the fat boy yelled. "I'm not going to jail. Even if I have to blow you apart to get out of this."

Jeb wanted to explain. To talk some sense into the boy. But there was no time. This kid was knotted up tighter than a funeral drum. No telling what might happen when Linda opened the door, which she was about to do right now!

Jeb did the only thing he could do. He picked up the eliminator. No point hurrying with a weapon already pointed at him. He'd either get a nasty death or Fat Boy would get rattled. He heard a hiss in the air, above him and to his left. No harm, no foul.

And a glimmer of hope. He might still talk some sense into the kid.

Then Linda opened the door. And Fat Boy swiveled the NA-One in her direction.

Jeb eliminated him.

Linda ran up. "The police should get here any time," she said. "I hit my panic button the second I walked in here."

But Jeb was staring at Fat Boy, who had just been reduced to a steaming blob. The NA-One still pointed from the robotic arm. A long reproachful finger.

Placing herself between Jeb and the carnage, Linda turned him away. She was eight inches shorter than he was, and fifty pounds lighter, but her grip on his shoulders was iron; she absolutely refused to let him look. "You had no choice," she said. Her voice was as gentle as a mother's kiss.

Jeb opened his mouth to speak, but the words stuck in his throat.

"Never a choice," Linda said. "You've got no reason to torment yourself over a forced decision." They both knew she wasn't talking about the boy he'd just eliminated. "Never mind," she said. "I've got no right." She reddened, and Jeb thought he'd never seen anything more beautiful.

"Things always improve when you show up," he said.

Linda took hold of his hand. "It's going to be alright," she said.

"Yeah," Jeb said. "I know it will."

Several seconds passed before he realized he was telling the truth.

POLYMER SCIENCE SUCKS

Kate Goodson was swimming against the current, fighting the roiling tide of Saturday night social norms. On a clear fall evening, when every student on the UMASS campus planned on being out all night, she was heading *back* to her dorm room.

She'd spent three hours studying in a quiet corner of a coffee shop, long enough (she hoped) for her roommate and the other girls on the hall to clear out. Some of them—those who didn't hook up—would be back in the wee hours of the morning. Forget sleep or sanity at that point. But Kate would indulge in some pleasure reading during the peaceful lull of their absence.

She'd downloaded a legal thriller by one of her favorite authors. None of that romantic bullshit. Fiction was imaginary, sure, but dwarfs and goblins were closer to reality than most love stories.

A typical Saturday night ... except for the prickly sensation of someone breathing down her neck. She was never eager to get back to the dorm. But her pace quickened to a brisk power walk. And the resulting burn in her legs prompted her to walk faster.

She paused at a call box. Looked around. Saw nothing. Except for the distant hum of traffic, she was all alone.

What the hell? She was almost there. So she didn't call for an escort. Didn't take her phone out of her purse either. But she did tighten her grip on the pepper-spray canister attached to her keychain.

Almost running now, she turned down the street lined with student housing. Her dorm was in sight. Her body unwound, tension rolling off of her, trickling harmlessly into the still night. She sighed. Took a deep breath. Savoring the crisp bite in the air.

Craziness. Jumping at ghosts. Worried about nothing.

Just a little bit further ...

The sudden whoosh of air sent her flying. Literally. It wasn't a tackle; she'd gotten launched. Kate sailed through the air and landed mercifully on lawn instead of the concrete.

"Oh, my word."

This was all wrong. A mugger or rapist was supposed to threaten you in a raspy hiss. This voice had no venom in it at all.

Kate's vision wavered out of focus, then cleared enough for her to see a boyish face, a face she thought she recognized. Professor Powell. A mild-mannered, mean-spirited asshole who gave out Ds by the handful, like candy at Halloween.

No way. It couldn't be. What would her toughest prof be doing here?

But somebody was kneeling next to her, patting her hand (which was beyond weird) and that somebody looked and sounded a lot like ...

What came next happened fast.

A scream caught in her throat.

An assailant loomed over them. A tall man in a yellow ski mask with black borders around the eyes and mouth; he looked like a professional wrestling heel. In his right hand was a small club or sawed-off bat, that he swung with a fury. It smashed against the back of the professor's skull with a sickening crack.

Sighing, Professor Powell (or whoever the hell this guy was) stood up and turned around in slow deliberation. "Now that wasn't very smart, was it?" he said.

Oh-my-God, Kate thought. *That's him.* Professor Powell loved to use that diminutive phrase when pointing out mistakes.

In this case, the villain, this masked wrestler, stood there with a shattered club in his hand, looking ridiculous. Then he sprinted away into the night.

Or he tried to.

The professor's bald head glittered in the twilight as he shot past the wrestler like a gilded cannonball and stumbled to a halt about twenty yards ahead of him.

Kate scrambled to her feet. The masked man had reversed course; he was running straight at her now. The professor was standing well back, shoulders slumped in disappointment.

Looking down, she realized she still had the pepper spray in her hand. The masked man got it full in the face. That put him on the ground. He was literally wallowing in pain, clutching his ski mask like a wounded dog.

Then another sudden whoosh. The wind almost knocked Kate off her feet. And an ensuing crash behind her sounded like a horrible traffic accident.

She backed away from her assailant, not daring to risk taking her eyes off of him to look behind her. "Are you alright?" she called.

No answer.

"Hello. Professor Powell?"

Nothing.

All she could do was dial 911 and keep a vigil, ready with more pepper spray if that dirtbag so much as twitched.

THE PROFESSOR WAS GONE when the police arrived. Two middle-aged campus cops, a male and a female, arrested the perpetrator (who was already wanted for other crimes). Then they got Kate's account of what had happened. Before she was halfway done, they were looking at her with bemused skepticism.

A nightstick or bat shattered on someone's head did sound pretty far-fetched—Kate had to admit it.

When she gave them Professor Powell's name as her rescuer, they offered to drive her to the infirmary for a quick checkup. After all, she'd had a shock.

Kate had to wonder about that herself.

Professor Powell! Really?

At any rate, she'd left out the part about the lightning-fast pursuit and the crash she'd heard. Winding up in a straightjacket wouldn't help her grade-point average or future career options beyond college.

EARLY SUNDAY MORNING, while her roommate was sleeping off a hangover, Kate went back to the exact same spot where it all happened. Standing alone in the wet grass, shivering in the cool intensity of the morning sun, she replayed the sequence of events in her head, letting herself relive the experience.

She watched her breath in the air, a white mist that lingered for a second before vanishing like Professor Powell. No. He didn't just vanish. But he'd been moving fast as hell. Too fast for her to follow with her eyes. Fast enough to create a serious air gust when he ran past her.

And the crash ... it had come from behind her.

Kate turned and started walking. She crossed the dew-soaked lawn and wound up in the parking lot next to Avery dorm. Nothing to see except a bunch of parked cars and a metal dumpster.

Okay. This was stupid. If anybody's car had been damaged last night, it would be all over social media by Monday at the latest. Or she could waste time and energy searching the parking lot for dented vehicles.

What the hell was she thinking anyhow? That Professor Powell—really, Professor Numb Nuts, of all people!—could actually damage something as formidable as a car with his body. Then again, hitting a deer, or even a dog, with your car could mean a trip to the body shop.

A thought struck her. Too ridiculous for words. Hell, beyond ridiculous. Transcending stupid and asinine. Kate walked over to the dumpster. It was army green, and large enough to hold a midsized car. Solid metal—with a huge dent in the side.

Kate's heart was pounding. This was the single biggest dent she'd ever seen. Nearly six feet high and half as wide. All one smooth indention too. No drunken Saturday night warrior with a sledgehammer could have done this. No way.

She could feel her ears pop from the pressure building

up inside of her. A combination of excitement and disbelief. And maybe a little fear mixed in for good measure.

The dent was almost human-shaped. It reminded her of a cartoon character running into a wall and leaving an imprint. Looking down, she saw two deep divots in the pavement. The collision had moved the dumpster a couple of feet.

"No way," Kate said aloud. "No way in hell."

KATE'S first class was at eight o'clock on Monday morning. Introduction to Polymer Engineering. Why she'd taken it was anybody's guess.

Polymer Science sucked.

She was hoping to graduate sooner rather than later—three years, to be exact. She wasn't a math major, but she understood the financial benefit of reducing her student loan by twenty-five percent. Still, after getting special permission to carry more than eighteen hours, why wouldn't she add on something easy?

No. Instead, she'd chosen to delve into the physical and mathematical principles required to solve engineering problems encountered with polymeric materials. And dropping the course was so not an option. Once Kate started something, she didn't quit. Period.

Worst of all, she'd wound up in Professor Powell's class. A brilliant scientist and researcher. A lousy teacher with zero people skills. Which didn't hurt him at all; it was his students who suffered in the form of ruined grade point averages.

Kate arrived early, took her seat on the front row, and tried to skim over her notes from last week, knowing it was hopeless after what had happened over the weekend. Forget about retaining anything in the upcoming lecture.

As the seats filled up around her and behind her, she stared at the blank chalkboard at the front of the room with new eyes. Professor Powell still used chalk—not presentations on the huge flatscreen, but chalk! This morning, however, that fresh blank chalkboard represented something of a clean slate. A whole new way of looking at a person she'd dismissed as a walking, talking rectum during the fall quarter.

Then Professor Powell arrived. And now, seeing him in person, in the light of day—Kate thought that maybe she *had* been delusional. A temporary psychosis bred from the trauma of being accosted. Add to that the feelings of alienation from her peers and the internal pressure she put on herself where goals were concerned. Assuming all of that was true—why her unconscious mind had imagined Professor Powell as her savior was anybody's guess. Freud would have had a meltdown over that one.

At any rate, the professor started writing on the chalkboard. Long-ass equations on the stress-strain analysis of solids. His chalk clacked against the board, producing that unmistakable smell of chalk in the air. Dust, in other words. Something you wouldn't get from a digital presentation.

The professor talked as he wrote. In a whiny Wikipedia voice, he just stated the facts with nary a hint of animation. No pausing to confirm that his class was still with him. No posing of questions to his students to keep them engaged. No interaction whatsoever. It was torture—like being locked in a room and forced to watch a documentary on dishwater.

Kate kept staring and wondered how in the hell this pudgy egghead could possibly shrug off a wooden bat to the skull or run too fast for words. Not that any mortal man should be able to do such things. But this guy ...

Yeah. Her mind had totally been pranking her.

Then she noticed something. When he reached for a fresh piece of chalk, his fingers looked ... wrong. Not wrong as in misshapen or deformed. They just didn't match *him*.

She looked closer, watching intently as the professor scrawled out more formulas. Professor Powell's hands ought to be soft and doughy. But these fingers looked strong and capable. Not quite slender, but certainly not the soft biscuits she'd expect from someone so physically unimposing as this guy.

Another thing ... when he turned to face the class, the shine that reflected off the top of his head. Here was a middle-aged man who was mostly bald except for a horseshoe of hair around the lower half of his head. She'd never noticed before—never had reason to notice—but bald men (even those not resorting to combovers) still had a layer of fuzz up top. Professor Powell's head had a shine to it. Clean shaven! What guy would shave the crown of his head and leave the rest untouched? Nobody would.

For the next half-hour, Kate chided herself for letting her imagination get away from her. But the more she stared at his hairline and watched him scrawl out his whirling matrix of incomprehensible equations on the chalkboard, the more she became convinced that she wasn't so delusional after all.

PROFESSOR POWELL KEPT regular office hours, but he'd made it clear from the get-go that he was not a tutor. So don't ask him about anything he'd already covered in class.

And all grades were final; no point in wasting his time and yours discussing it. In other words, he was physically there, as in butt in a seat behind his desk; but forget about having a real conversation, much-less assistance with anything class related—kinda the whole point of office hours in the first place.

That worked to Kate's advantage because nobody ever showed up at his office. No point. Unless you just liked getting pissed off and frustrated.

Which meant that she could get the professor alone. He looked surprised—even shocked—when she waltzed right into his office and shut the door behind her. Recognition flashed across his face, followed by a hostile stare.

Kate helped herself to a chair in front of his desk. "I know it was you," she said. No point beating around the bush. "Saturday night. You saved me from getting attacked."

The professor's face reddened. "If this is some sort of prank, I am *not* amused," he said.

"I didn't believe it at first."

"Leave my office. Now."

Kate stood up. "Fine. I wasn't going to post the video without your permission. But screw it now." She turned to leave.

"Ms. Goodson. Pause a moment." The professor's eyelids narrowed into slits of concentration. He was clearly deep in thought as if she wasn't even in the room. Finally, after a long stretch of silence, he opened his eyes and stared daggers at Kate. "This video footage you speak of? It's nonexistent. Please leave my office now."

Kate's face got hot. But she clamped her teeth together, determined not to respond. No. Not yet.

"And furthermore," he said. "I highly recommend that you drop my class and save yourself a lot of wasted effort."

"That's it?" Kate said. "That's all you've got to say?"

"Goodbye, Ms. Goodson."

Instead of leaving, Kate sat down again. She'd never played a hand of poker in her life. But it didn't take a genius to realize (at least intuitively) that if you were going to bluff, you'd better be prepared to go all the way with it.

"You're right about one thing," she said. "I didn't take any video on my phone. You probably noticed. I was way too busy for that at the time. But I'll bet you didn't know about the video cameras covering the side parking lot of Avery dorm."

She watched the professor's face go slack and pale. This guy was a highly respected research scientist. A brilliant mind. But not a poker player at all.

Kate pressed her advantage. "That parking lot is lit up pretty well at night. Even the area around the dumpster."

Professor Powell patted his face with a handkerchief. "I'm going to pretend this conversation never happened," he said. "The very fact that you gained access to any video footage—which happens to be university property—constitutes an honors violation. We're talking expulsion here, Ms. Goodson. Do you understand?"

"What I understand is your face shows up on camera clear as day," Kate said. "We had to enhance the image, me and a friend of mine in the computer lab. But it's you crashing into that dumpster. Not even a question there."

The professor looked away. She'd made him break eye contact. "I suppose you plan to post your little film clip on social media," he said. "That would be a big mistake on your part. Obtaining that video footage is the same as stealing books from the library or furniture from your dormitory. Not only will your education come to a screeching halt, you'll face criminal charges as well. I'll see to that."

It might have ended right there. In that moment, Kate almost left Professor Powell's office and proceeded to drop his class. Cease and desist. Move on with her life. This guy was a horse's ass in the nth degree. Let him keep his secret if that made him happy.

But he'd pissed her off. Kate was no longer intimidated. Still—a self-preservation instinct in the back of her mind sent up a warning flare. *Don't be stupid.* After all, this guy was a highly respected faculty member, virtually un-fire-able, who just might have superhuman abilities. Not someone to push too far.

"I'm not posting anything anywhere," she said. "I only want one thing."

The professor folded his hands on the desk in front of him and nodded at her to proceed.

"Tell me the truth about Saturday night," Kate said.

"I assume that's your non-negotiable price for that alleged video in your possession," Professor Powell said.

"You'll never have to worry about that. Just quit bull-shitting me."

They sat in full silence for about half a minute, eyes locked, taking stock of one another.

"Get out of my office," Professor Powell said.

Maybe he *had* played poker before.

THE RIOT HAPPENED one week later.

It began as a crowd of protesters. Something about banning inappropriate books. No cause for alarm there. Protests in Western Massachusetts were as routine as high tea in London.

But when a dozen more demonstrators showed up in

riot gear—helmets, camouflage, and heavy boots—things escalated from a hum to a rumble, from a few pebbles to a thundering avalanche.

Kate was in the library, still nursing the remnants of a hangover. It was Monday afternoon, one week to the day after her ill-fated visit to Professor Powell. Last weekend, she'd decided to hang out with Annie and the party crowd. No stay-at-home book reading. This girl needed a change. It was a decision she'd been regretting all day.

The past weekend hadn't been particularly fun, just a haze of drunken insanity. She remembered enough to know that she hadn't done anything overly stupid. And nothing else about the weekend was really worth remembering. Maybe that's why drunks suffered memory loss; they never did anything worth remembering. Better to just erase the mental blackboard and start over.

Speaking of erasures, her schedule had gotten softer, compliments of dropping Intro to Polymer Engineering. And speaking of softer, if the wooden chair she was sitting in had been a cushioned recliner, she would have dozed off an hour ago. She'd press on for a little while longer. Wrap up her reading for Business Law, then go home and take a nap. Maybe she'd wake up and realize the last ten days had been a weird dream. She could hope, anyhow.

An uneasy feeling tickled the back of her neck. Kate sensed that she was being watched. Casting a quick glance over her shoulder, she saw Professor Powell walking away from her. How weird was that? She would have expected him to frequent the Science and Engineering Library on Pleasant Street. Not this branch.

Whatever. Like she cared.

Kate thought she might flip him off if he walked by her again, then reminded herself to not be stupid. Faculty member. Might have superpowers. Don't push it. In fact, screw it for today. She was going back to the dorm for that nap right now.

Then all hell broke loose.

Alarms started going off. Loud bells accompanied by foghorn blasts. Good luck trying to hear yourself think with that racket. Kate guessed that some moron tripped a fire alarm.

The alarms stopped. A strident female voice spoke over the intercom. "Attention students. Operating out of an abundance of caution, we have locked down the library for the next hour."

Locked down, Kate thought. *What the hell?*

"Do not try to leave this building. All doors have been locked. The security system has been engaged. Campus police have been notified."

The voice wasn't a live person. They actually recorded stuff like this in anticipation of shit inevitably hitting the fan.

Within minutes, most of the students inside had gathered at the front entrance. Probably about fifty in all. Kate climbed on top of the circulation desk for a better look. The librarian in charge didn't utter a word of protest. Understandably so. The spectacle outside was downright creepy.

There were at least a hundred batshit-crazy people. Kate noticed a couple of overturned cars across the street. And the noise. It was the rumble of a great beast. As if the mob had become a single entity. A hive mind.

A hush settled over everybody inside. A collective fear. If those nut jobs outside were predators, they were prey. Sucked to be on this side of the glass.

Kate felt a helpless fear. That fateful Saturday night incident didn't compare to this shit. Then, she'd been scared and panicked, but not totally helpless (at least from her perspective). Now she was a goldfish surrounded by a school of piranhas.

Her mind screamed at her to run. But her legs were concrete. She just stood there like a useless lump, watching in disbelief as the throng of rioters swarmed up the library steps. This was what it was like to be mesmerized by your own helplessness.

Mercifully, they paused at the doors. One of the ringleaders shouted through a bullhorn; that got them chanting, gathering steam for something bigger. The inevitable brick bounced off one of the glass doors. Not good. Kate couldn't grasp Polymer Engineering, but she did know that breakproof glass could be broken.

In the face of this escalating tempest of humanity, Kate barely noticed the activity going on around her. About a dozen male students were hauling study tables to the front entrance. They were leaning them against the doors.

Thankfully, that snapped Kate out of her terrified funk. She rushed to help with the makeshift barricade, stacking chairs, pushing desks. It was going to be okay. They were walling themselves in behind an improvised fort.

Then came the thuds—one behind another—followed by the unmistakable crash of broken glass. Things got worse really fast. The wall of tables started to tip inward.

Students and faculty on the inside rallied to support their barricade. Some sat on desks to anchor the base; others leaned against the makeshift walls, hoping to keep them upright. But the pounding and thudding were relentless.

Kate felt the desk she was sitting on start to slide. The thudding sent shockwaves down her legs and up the base of her spine. And the proximity of the mob outside, their collective ire, the sheer power of their combined force, took her breath away.

Reinforcements arrived. More people with more furniture. Chairs, end tables, even heavy books. Kate hopped down off the desk to make room but knew it was too little, too late.

Unless ...

Where the hell was Professor Powell?

KATE RAN in the general direction she'd seen Professor Powell going just a short while ago. She'd never realized it before—never had a reason to—but finding somebody in a library was hard. With row after row of tall shelves filled with books, not to mention all of the cubbies and cubicles off to the side, it was like searching a maze.

Well, duh. This place was designed for privacy, after all. Which did give her some options. If those crazies got in here, she could hide out in the stacks. But that wouldn't help those people at the entrance.

The problem was ... where to even start looking. There were twenty-eight floors to pick from. Twenty-eight floors! Yeah, this building just happened to hold the record for *Tallest Library in the World.*

Which also meant that rounding up those rioters, if they got inside, could be a huge job for law enforcement. She had to find Professor Powell. But how?

Kate stopped near the first-floor elevator bank, with no clue on how to proceed. Did she cover this first floor? Did she start at the top and work down? Find a safe place to hide? Go back and help at the entrance? Tears sprang to her eyes. Indecision was for the weak and helpless like her mom. She couldn't give in. No way. Even though this past week had been one defeat after another.

She swiped at her nose with the back of her hand as the first tears began to flow. Rivers of frustration. Streams of failure. She couldn't ...

"Ms. Goodson."

Professor Powell! He'd walked up to her. He was standing right there with a book in his hand. Kate let out a yelp of relief and had to restrain herself from hugging him. "C'mon," she said. "We need you."

The professor responded with a blank stare.

"Didn't you hear me?" Kate knew her voice was harsh and edgy. But screw it. "There's a crazed mob outside and they're busting in."

"I suggest sequestering yourself in a safe place."

Kate grabbed his arm, then released it. The professor's deadpan expression didn't falter. A statue would have been more responsive. "We can stop them," she said. "*You* can stop them."

"Not my concern," he said.

"Hey. I know you don't want anybody to find out about ... your powers, or whatever you've got. But you could just push against the barricade and keep it from moving. Nobody has to know you were anything more than a warm body."

The professor turned away.

Kate slapped the book out of his hand. A romance novel, the kind of book that winds up as a made-for-TV movie. This guy was full of surprises.

"Seriously," she said. "People are going to get hurt. This place is going to be trashed. You could stop it. But no. You're going to hide in a corner and read this crap."

Professor Powell just picked up his book and walked away.

"You asshole!" Kate shrieked. She wanted to jump on his back and dig her nails into his face. Instead, she yelled after him. "You're a lousy human being."

Then she sprinted back to the front entrance.

GLASS FRAGMENTS RAINED DOWN like silver daggers. Slowly but inevitably, the protective wall of library furniture was being pushed backward.

Turning her back to the entrance, Kate pressed her butt against a desk and pushed for all she was worth. But her shoes slid across the tile floor in fits and starts, losing a little more purchase with every succession of thuds from the mob outside.

She made momentary eye contact with the guy next to her, a stout redhead with pale skin. "Doesn't have to be this way," she muttered.

"*They* think it does," he said.

No point in trying to explain that she'd been referring to Professor Powell, Asshole Meritorious. Besides, there were more pressing matters facing them at the moment.

The barricade slid inward. One of the tables fell crashing to the floor. The next few seconds were critical. They could either make a run for it or stand aside and hope those lunatics left them alone to focus on whatever vandalism they had in mind.

A bad scene that didn't have to be that way. Unnecessary loss that could have been avoided. But no. Some distinguished dickwad couldn't be bothered …

Kate quit thinking. She urged her burning legs to push harder.

Next thing she knew, she was on her butt. The barricade had disappeared from under her, and she was pushing air.

She heard crashes. At least two of them. Loud. With solid impact. The shouts of the rioters had gone silent. The stuffy air inside the library, wrought with heat and tension, had been replaced by a crisp fall breeze.

Kate looked over her shoulder. Then she scrambled to her feet and gaped at the wide-open entrance where glass doors *used* to be. Camouflaged bodies of rioters littered the brick entryway. And fifty yards away on the sidewalk, a study table was lodged in the side of a capsized car.

Maybe the professor wasn't a total asshole after all.

PROFESSOR POWELL LIVED in a ranch-style house on top of a hill about three miles from campus. Kate sat at his kitchen table with a steaming mug of green tea in front of her. The view of the Holyoke Mountain range through his back windows was spectacular. Especially with the setting sun behind them, a welcome curtain falling on another day of turmoil.

Yesterday's library siege had been the main story on the local news, also garnering national attention. Already, over twenty people had been arrested. Video footage from the outside cameras made for easy identification of the rioters. And to further simplify the process, eleven of the ringleaders had been conveniently incapacitated when Professor Powell surged through the doors.

Still—the state police took everybody's name and contact info. More than just protocol, Kate assumed. They'd be asking a lot of questions. And Kate knew she was going to lie her ass off.

"I really don't think they'll figure out it was you," Kate said.

Professor Powell raised a questioning eyebrow. "Based on what, Ms. Goodson? Your experience as a master criminal?"

Kate sipped her honey-sweetened tea, reminding herself that the professor's abrasiveness wasn't a personal affront. "I'm basing it on the video footage," she said. "You know. That clip that's gone viral." She could be condescending too when it suited her.

Said video featured the shirtless body of a total stud. A human bulldozer with a study table as its front blade. Furthermore, the professor had had the foresight to wear his shirt over his head.

Please don't make me say it, Kate thought. She really didn't want to tell him that nobody in their wildest imaginings would ever associate that pumped up, superhuman specimen with a talking tub of jello like himself.

"My concern lies with the library's video footage in its entirety," the professor said. "No doubt they captured me going inside before the chaos erupted. And a close examination will reveal that I never leave."

"They'll never make the connection," Kate said. "They'll identify you as a mild-mannered, law-abiding faculty member, and move on. Even without a clip of you leaving ... I mean, look in the mirror. The possibility of you being that unknown hero would never come up in a million years."

The professor pulled up his shirt and revealed an inflatable life vest. Something like a smile flitted across his face.

"You're referring to my enhanced girth," he said. "Before making my grand entrance yesterday, I deflated my camouflage and shoved it down the front of my pants. Additional enhancement, I suppose."

Kate chewed her lip, still expecting a blaring alarm clock to wake her out of this weird dream. "How long have you been covering up your ... stud-li-ness?" she asked.

"About three months, give or take."

"Wait a minute. You've been at UMASS for at least—"

"Twelve years next March," the professor said.

"I don't get it. How did you suddenly go from ..."

"Blimp to stud," the professor supplied. "We still haven't gotten to polymer processing in class. And based on your test results before you dropped out ... never mind. What do you know about stem cell generation?"

"Not a damn thing."

"Very well," The professor said. "I'll simplify it for you. Stem cells contribute to muscle formation and regeneration from injury."

"So?"

"Well, a deceased colleague of mine in the biology department left behind reams of research that nobody knew about. I came upon this material—actually, never mind the how or why of it—he was able to map out how a cell's gene network changes during a person's lifetime."

Kate's eyes glazed over.

"From there, we're talking about the possibility of generating skeletal muscle cells from human stem cells."

"I have no clue what you just said."

The professor stared at the tabletop as if he wanted to pound his head on it. "It's possible to develop muscle stem cells in the lab that have the ability to self-renew and develop in the human body."

"I didn't know biology was your thing," Kate said.

"You think polymers *aren't* living matter?" the professor said. "Self-repairing plastic is no new discovery by any stretch."

"What you're saying is: combining your research with somebody else's, you turned yourself into a human guinea pig, and it backfired."

The professor's head reddened for a moment. He cleared his throat and averted his eyes. "In a word: yes."

"Holy shit! You made a cocktail and shot yourself up."

"Nothing so daring or dramatic as that," the professor said. "I was attempting to create a no-chip nail polish and launch my own product line."

"And?"

"And I'm jerking your chain. Of course, I injected myself. An IV bag with a controlled drip. When I woke up four days later—"

"You passed out for four days! Did you know it was going to be that dangerous?"

The professor walked over to the window and gazed out at the sun setting behind the mountains. "I was going through a rough patch. A dark time. I suppose I just didn't care."

Kate walked over to him, resisting the urge to hug this un-huggable cactus of a human being. "So what happened?"

"I should think that's obvious," he said. "Between my bones becoming stronger than the material used to build jet planes and my muscle fiber breaking down and repairing itself without any physical exertion on my part—"

"No! I mean—are you alright?"

"Of course. Aside from the fact that I have an insatiable appetite. And I have to keep up appearances. That's imperative. Hence, the faux stomach and baldness. My career will be ruined if this ever becomes known."

Kate grabbed his hands, squeezing too hard. "I'm talking about your mental health, you asshole." The *respected faculty, superhuman, don't be stupid* reminder pinged her brain. *Whatever,* she responded back to herself. "Look. Any way you slice and dice it, we're talking suicide attempt. Injecting yourself like that is no different than putting a gun to your head."

The professor freed his hands from Kate's with a gentle pull. Then he took the empty tea mugs into his neat and orderly kitchen.

Kate followed him. "You can't go around like my—look, you've gotta talk about your shit. With somebody. Period."

The professor was standing at the sink, washing the mugs, and staring straight ahead at nothing.

"Did you hear what I just said?" Kate demanded.

"I'm not suicidal, Ms. Goodson," he said. "I merely happened to value a landmark scientific breakthrough above my own wellbeing. That's all."

"Unbelievable." Taking deep breaths, Kate willed herself not to go off on this stupid, arrogant ...

"Hope it was worth it," she said.

The professor favored her with a sad smile. "It wasn't," he said. "The experiment was a failure. And now I'm stuck in this ridiculous—"

"Whoa! Hold up. Failure? You're a freaking superhero."

The professor responded in the didactic voice he used in class. "Suppose you were to put an old lady who's never driven over the speed limit on the NASCAR circuit," he said. "She'd have all the necessary equipment. What would be the problem?"

"Not the same thing," Kate said.

"Isn't it? I have no control over the amount of force I exert. It's like running a faucet wide open or shutting it off. No in between whatsoever."

"Look at what you're doing now," Kate said.

They both stared at the mug in the professor's hand.

"You haven't broken it or flung it across the room. And you write just fine on the blackboard without punching a hole in it."

"Hardly the same thing," the professor said. But his voice lacked conviction.

"Don't you see?" Kate's voice quivered with excitement. "Dishwashing, writing on blackboards, probably all kinds of lab stuff with beakers and other breakable shit. These are things you've done over and over for years."

"By rote," the professor said.

"Sure. So how often did you ever run at full speed? Or sling something heavy around?"

Professor Powell's face went slack. "Ms. Goodson! That's the answer. That's the answer!"

SKINNER STATE PARK.

Early on a Tuesday morning. Dew glistened off the yellow and white pines. The more colorful trees were barely starting to turn. When they did, creating a fire burst of elm, ash, and red maple, this trail, and all others around here, would be too crowded for their purposes.

The trail started where Route 47 ran along the base of the mountain. "Okay," Kate had softly encouraged. "Easy jog up." Right. Up! That trail went *straight up*. Kinda the idea in this case.

As she drove up the mountain towards the ranger's

station, Kate heard a thunderous crash in the woods below. But Professor Powell was waiting for her when she got there. He wore jeans, a flannel shirt, and skullcap. Also sunglasses.

His book bag was sitting on the passenger seat of Kate's Honda Civic. A book bag with several thick books on the science of kinetics—exercise science, in other words. As if that was going to help him. As if he'd be able to think his way through the process. Which wasn't as bizarre as it seemed—Kate had to admit. After all, this was a man who'd been thinking his way around, over, and through problems and puzzles his entire life.

Kate stopped the car and lowered the window. "I'm afraid I'm still a bull in a china shop," the professor said. His clothes were ripped in the chest and legs. Kate pitied the tree he'd run into on (or off) the trail below.

They were one level above the base of the mountain. From here, the road kicked up into an incline worthy of a mountain stage in the Tour de France. Straight up for half a mile, then a sharp hairpin curve.

Kate hefted the thickest book and handed it to the professor. "Try reading while you're walking," she suggested. "Should be familiar. I've seen you doing that on your way to class. When you get in a rhythm, kick the pace a little."

Opening the book, Professor Powell paused. "Why are you spending your time helping me, Ms. Goodson?"

"Are you kidding? This is special. Totally insane. Over the top dangerous. But special."

"You know, this is not the birth of a superhero," the professor said. "This is a scientific study. Nothing more."

"Just stick your nose in the book and get going," Kate said.

Maybe this *was* just a bullshit exercise. Maybe the professor really would be content to just gain knowledge for the sake of knowledge. Or maybe that anonymous stud with his head shrouded to hide his identity would make another appearance.

One could only hope.

"Ms. Goodson. You're welcome back in my class anytime."

"Thanks, Professor." Kate flashed her brightest smile. "But Polymer Science sucks."

PICTURE THIS

Privacy versus disclosure. Technology had created this dilemma by evolving faster than society itself. So, in turn, it was up to technology to offer a compromise.

And Marjorie Dunlap sat alone in her dorm room, browsing through that compromise on her phone. Well, not really browsing. She'd received a single upload request from a total stranger: a photo of a male coed with his visiting parents. Because Marjorie could be seen in the background —compliments of advanced face recognition algorithms—a bitwise NOT code prevented the photo from being uploaded, copied, or printed without her consent.

Before Marjorie could tap her approval, the door flew open and her roommate, Alice, burst into the room. "I just got asked to the spring formal," she said, barely able to keep the squeal out of her voice.

"Really? Who's the guy?"

"Nobody you'd know ... Trey Windholm."

"I know who he is," Marjorie said.

"I was sitting in the student union all by myself. Then I

looked up and he was sitting right across from me. Oh my God, he has the most gorgeous blue eyes."

Marjorie let a heavy sigh escape. Heavier than she realized.

"Try not to get *too* excited for me!" Alice snapped.

"Sorry ..." Marjorie offered. "Hey, that's great."

"You know, if I was as negative as you are, I'd kill myself!"

Marjorie shrugged. "You may be right," she said. Her prepackaged response that she used to end arguments before they started. After all, how could anyone disagree with that simple statement without admitting they were full of shit?

And it worked. Alice slammed the door on her way out.

Marjorie sighed again. What Alice didn't know was that Trey Windholm *and* Billy Cobb *and* Keith Williams—all Omega-Omicrons—had asked her—Marjorie!—to the spring formal yesterday. And one thing was certain: guys didn't wake up interested in her or Alice.

Because Marjorie Dunlap knew. Any attempt to improve her appearance yielded the same result: she looked worse. Rouge accentuated her meaty jowls. Eyeliner drew attention to her bulbous nose. With no makeup at all, her skin had the pallor of sour pudding. And her hair ...she always left a salon looking worse than before she went in. Wardrobe choices didn't help either. Form fitting clothes exposed her obesity. Loose garments made her look like a walking tent. So she'd given up trying to be attractive at all. And the result: she looked worse.

Granted, horse-faced, straw-haired Alice was perhaps less unpleasant to look at, if your taste favored scarecrow over blob. Still ...

She spoke into her phone. "Trey Windholm. Profile

Page." And the first thing that popped up was a hologram of his girlfriend: one drop-dead gorgeous Kelli Monroe. High cheekbones, ski-slope nose, brown eyes, lustrous black hair. All on a hot little body that made the guy's heads swivel as she walked past them.

So connect those dots for me, Alice ...

FOR THE REST of the week, Marjorie remembered to indulge Alice with a nod and an occasional smile as she prattled on about her upcoming *hot date*. Even though it felt like she was giving a big thumbs-up to someone about to jump out of a plane without a parachute.

Then Friday night rolled around. Alice got cozy with a bottle of vodka. Except, this time, she remained in their room. Apparently, her elevated social status ruled out prowling the bars for guys too wasted to care what they did or who they did it with.

Marjorie wanted to shake her awake. To scream at her!

Here was a homely girl being offered a banana peel disguised as Cinderella's slipper ... what *was* their game?

Why did she care? Whatever humiliation those Omega jerks had in store for Alice would come with built-in containment. Illegal activity—including harassment, bully-ing, intimidation—was exempt from privacy protection. That meant dumping a vat of pig's blood on a hapless victim (like they did in that old movie, *Carrie*) could be photographed or recorded and sent to the authorities. No approval taps needed.

Consequently, from kindergarten onward, the popular cliques had no misfits to dump on. Couldn't upload photos of them, nor write nasty comments about them. Abuse them on the playground, and you ran the risk of someone filming the incident.

Marjorie had read the stories from previous decades about the cruelty of cyberbullying, about teens slitting their wrists, about how lucky she was to live in a society of transparency, where behavior and accountability went hand in hand.

She'd never been bullied. Not even once. Still, part of her couldn't help thinking that a little persecution might have been nice. Acknowledgement that she existed, if nothing else.

MARJORIE FELL in love with old school photography during high school. Having no friends to distract her, and because her grandfather, who just happened to be a photography buff, moved in with the family in lieu of a retirement center, she learned how to develop film in a darkroom. Actual glossy photos that you pasted in a scrapbook.

Everything one hundred percent mechanical. A lens directed light; the film provided a chemical element for storing the image; and the camera itself ... nothing more than a box that kept the lens and film apart until a shutter opened and closed.

No phones, no upload requests. No people either. Most of her photos were of wildlife, landscapes, and sunsets.

Forget about pointing your phone in a vague direction and clicking off a dozen shots. Not only was each vintage photo a significant time and energy investment, but a roll of film (expensive and scarce nowadays) had a limited number of prints. For Marjorie, that was part of the allure. The challenge of framing her shot, of planning around the lighting available. Of knowing that she had one chance to capture a moment in time.

RUDY TOLLIVER, an Omega pledge, was talking to a rugged girl who resembled a longshoreman. Marjorie walked up just in time to catch the final snippets of their conversation. Rudy asked the girl to the social, and she informed him that she wasn't into guys, even platonically.

Marjorie was waiting when he turned around. With an idea in her head. An idea evolving into a plan. "I'll go with you," she said.

"Oh-my-God, thanks Marjorie. That's awesome!" Rudy had the look of a drowning man who'd been thrown a life preserver.

Marjorie gave him a cold smile. *Yeah, I'm Miss Popularity.*

SO NOW, Alice and Marjorie were waiting in the lobby of their dorm. They'd received separate texts from their dates informing them that a cab would pick them up at 7:oo PM sharp.

Marjorie wore jeans and a heavy sweater. Her only accessory was a fanny pack, which housed her old-fashioned camera.

"Jesus, Marjorie," Alice snorted in disgust. "You could at least try to look presentable."

To which Marjorie replied: "You may be right."

She'd watered down Alice's booze and replaced her anxiety meds with sugar pills that would hopefully look like the real thing to a drunken person. Whatever happened, Marjorie didn't want her doing anything foolish. Bad enough that Alice had overpaid a hair stylist for highlights and a body wave; the result was a frizzy limpness that made her appear destitute. And her new dress with the bright floral print only accentuated her drabness. Especially with the extra padding in the chest ... it was like trying to dress up a mop as a storefront mannequin.

When two cabs showed up—one for each girl—Marjorie knew the Omegas were keeping them apart for a reason. Whatever their plan, it was elaborate and expensive.

Their destination was the Belhaven, a luxury hotel five miles from campus. Away from the mainstream. It boasted a large conference room, often used for wedding receptions and business functions.

Marjorie's driver merged into a line of at least twenty other cabs. One at a time, each of them dropped off a single passenger and drove away.

As her own cab neared the drop-off point, Marjorie could see the girls ahead of her getting out. And every last one of them was unattractive—no, downright ugly!

Her resolve evaporated. A sense of dread churned in her stomach. The camera hung heavy in her fanny pack, a useless lump of metal.

No way in hell she'd be able to leave the refuge of this back seat ...

Go now!

An inner voice—a push, a shout—got her hand on the door handle. Ignoring the driver's protest, she exited the cab and headed straight to the door. On her way, she removed the camera from her fanny pack.

No plan. Except that it had to happen now. Before she lost her nerve.

MARJORIE OPENED THE DOOR. The first thing she noticed was the room's brightness—good for photos—that and the stench of sweat and puke that accompanied drunkenness.

A misshapen girl with a gourd-shaped butt and a face torched by acne had entered ahead of her. And a tuxedo-clad Omega was ushering her to a set of steps that led to an elevated stage.

The emcee's amplified voice announced them. *Ms. Kimberly Overton, escorted by Mr. Mark Johnson.* Marjorie stared slack-jawed as the Omega walked his "date" across the stage. Their entrance was blanketed by hoots and guffaws ... directed *not* at the girl, but at the Omega himself. *Looking good, Mark. You're a real stud. I wanna be you.*

Of course, anybody witnessing this spectacle would easily surmise what was going on. This was a dog fight. An ugly date contest. With complete impunity for the Omegas.

Their defense rested on a hairline, but it rested nonetheless. There was nothing illegal, immoral, or cruel about escorting a girl to an event. And the taunts and jeers were directed at the Omega himself. All in fun, he could say. Nothing hurtful. Just my people roasting me a little. Translation: this spectacle couldn't be posted without his approval. Meaning that none of this was actually happening. At least not in a damaging context.

Something else: the shriek of female laughter. The Omega's sister sorority was in on this too ...

Marjorie raised her camera and paused. She'd entered the banquet hall through a side door, which, from a photographer's perspective, split the room into two separate frames ... meaning she could either photograph the pimply girl onstage or the jeering sorority girls in the audience. And she really needed both in the same photo.

One further complication: Rudy, her own date, had spotted her. Marjorie sidled away as he approached, and also scanned the room through the viewfinder on her camera.

Click.

She captured the moment. The abashed girl onstage fluctuating between denial and realization as the girls in the audience bombarded her date (right, not her) with pig calls.

Click.

Another frozen moment. Pain and bewilderment in the face of heartless derision.

If only ...

Click.

She caught it all in the same photo. The Omega's humiliated victim, plus Kelli Monroe—gorgeous fucking Kelli—exhorting her female cohorts to a new level of ridicule.

Click. Gotcha, queen bitch.

SHE WASN'T one for fantasy. But Marjorie had been imagining how it would go ever since her photos came to life on the glossy paper.

Her bomb would drop in a very public place. And today, that place was the snack bar in the student center. Kelli was sitting at a table across the room, surrounded by her clique of girlfriends. And Trey Windholm was there as well. An added bonus.

With a cool triumph that comes from having the winning hand, Marjorie would walk up and plop a thick envelope down in front of Kelli. She'd say: "You really need to look at this."

And as the queen bitch thumbed through the photos, her face would knot up into a pretty scowl. Then she'd respond: "This is highly illegal. I never approved any of these images."

And Marjorie would tell her to do an online search on photography, as in *the process of transferring images from film to glossy paper*. That, and the concept of unlimited copies for whoever owned the negatives.

She imagined Kelli's haughty rebut. "Well, you can't share them anywhere."

Then the coup de grâce: "Actually, snail mail still exists for packages. And all your info is right there for me in cyberspace. So there's nothing stopping me from mailing these photos to the CEO of any organization you wind up working for. And maybe your future in-laws could stand some enlightenment."

So what was she waiting for?

All she had to do was waddle across the snack bar—less than ten yards—and settle the score. Yes. Get even ...

At the social, Rudy had walked up to her and offered his arm—undaunted by the obvious fact that she'd just witnessed everything. And oblivious to the danger of her picture taking. He'd assumed she'd been using a digital device that required approval clicks for posting.

The problem—her problem—had started there. Because at that moment, that part of her that craved acceptance, the Alice in her, yearned to take his arm and be escorted across the stage. Even knowing it was the virtual equivalent of a moth being drawn to the light of a flame that would burn it to a cinder.

And now growing in its place, in that hole left inside of

her ... malice. Resentment. A bitterness toward anyone more attractive than herself—the whole damn world, in other words.

She glared across the room at Kelli and Trey. They were happily oblivious, while she was seething. It was like drinking poison and hoping the person you were mad at would die.

Well, that was about to change.

She slid the envelope into the trash as she headed outside. Letting go of that damn anchor!

She'd hang onto the negatives, just in case. *Right. For how long? The next* 100 *years?*

Nope. Some things she couldn't afford.

She smiled when she heard Alice's voice in her head. *Defeatist cow!*

"You may be right," she said aloud.

Thank you for reading my book! If you are new to my writing, I really appreciate you giving this book a try. I hope I kept you turning the pages and gave you an entertaining reading experience.

And to my awesome repeat readers: thanks so much for your continued support.

If you enjoyed the book, I would be incredibly grateful if you left a review. It really helps a lot.

Stay in the loop!

Join my mailing list to keep up with my new releases, promos, and free offerings. (Who doesn't like free stuff?)

https://bonnerlitchfield.com

But wait! There's more. Keep reading for a sneak peek at another one of my books.

Again, thanks for reading!

**Keep reading for an
exciting excerpt from *Space Hack*.**

ONE

Kevin stood at the edge of the hangar bay, all alone. The fact that he was down here by himself should have been reassuring. That meant nobody on the ship knew his whereabouts at the moment. But the still silence screamed at him to run. And every part of him agreed. A prickly apprehension ran up his spine. His knees trembled as he willed himself to breathe.

The massive hangar was shaped like a honeycomb, larger than a gymnasium or even an outdoor playing field. High overhead, a solid white glow illuminated everything.

Each wall was comprised of cog-shaped steel plates that interlocked like puzzle pieces. Huge silver floor tiles, cold and solid under Kevin's boots, spread out before him in a symmetric pattern of gleaming rectangles. Kevin figured each tile to be fifty times his mass. If he hadn't felt puny and insignificant before, he did now.

The hawkers—single-person fighters—were lined up in the center of the hangar. Two hundred of them, arranged in ten uniform rows. Waiting for a command to get things started. Basking in the glow from the ceiling, each one was a swift predator with a single black eye and a sleek white body with red trim.

They all seemed to be staring at Kevin, mocking him, threatening, anticipating his next move. In fact, the hangar felt like a giant booby trap ready to grind his bones to a powder if he dared to take a single step forward.

These thoughts were just imaginary bullshit in his head, sure, but they were also byproducts of his fear. Thoughts could be dispelled; cowardice, not so much.

Even the lightweight body armor he was wearing was no help. This was a suit that turned average dudes into studs. Black and imposing, it bulged out in all the right places and made the wearer look like a superhero. Or an imposter. Even though it had been custom fitted to his slight frame, putting it on always made Kevin feel like a worm in a snake's skin.

And that made all the difference. Other recruits got reckless when they wore the armor. Kevin stayed scared. He'd never worked up the nerve to launch himself at a target with full abandon, always fearful of the impact. The possibility of a bruise or a sprain made him want to puke.

As did wearing his helmet right now. With the dark face shield almost touching his nose, the smell of neoprene—that and knowing he was breathing filtered air—gave Kevin a sense of drowning. The slightest malfunction, the tiniest crack or compromise, a pinhole-sized opening anywhere, and he was a goner. Never mind that the hangar was sealed tight as a drum, that he could walk in here naked as the day he was born and breathe just fine.

Even his weapon felt heavy and useless, hanging on his right hip like an extra appendage. A painful reminder of his ineptitude in the practice simulator, and validation that he didn't belong. Small wonder that he always got singled out during drills. And small wonder that he couldn't hope to do what he'd come down here for.

Directly behind him next to the door he'd just come through, the palm reader's red circle dared him to set his plan in motion. One touch. That's all it would take. The thick metal doors on the other side of the room would slide apart. The hawker of his choice would be Kevin's to command.

Except—his lack of manhood had rendered him immobile. Hell, his boots, for all intents and purposes, were welded to the metal floor. Unable to press on. Unable to turn tail and run. He stared at his feet, searching for an answer in the polished chrome.

A soft hand on his shoulder made him cower and yelp. Worse still was the echo of his own voice inside his helmet. Hearing himself squeal like a little girl was beyond demeaning.

"Relax, Kevin."

His blood raced when he recognized the girl's voice. Tonya Verdi. She was wearing the same black combat gear as Kevin with one huge difference: her body enhanced the armor, not the other way around. With her face shield raised, her bronzed skin glowed in the white light. Her easy smile caused gooseflesh on Kevin's skin, followed by a surge of hopeful lust that he immediately dismissed as impossible fantasy.

Tonya gave his shoulder a reassuring squeeze.

"Wh-what are you doing here?" Kevin stammered.

Her brown eyes had a flirtatious gleam, as if sneaking into a restricted area was just a lark. "I could ask you the same thing," she said.

"Nothing." Kevin looked down and wished the massive floor tiles would swallow him up. "Nothing at all."

<h1 style="text-align:center">TWO</h1>

Join the Armada!

Seemed like a good idea at the time.

In Kevin's homeland, some folks mined carbon. Others worked on assembly lines building nanotubes for circuit boards. All of them low-paid grunts. His mother took great pride in never having missed a shift in twenty years.

Consequently, nobody there cared a whit for logic or abstract thought. No call for people who could embed instructions into those nanotubes they manufactured. No. Cushy work of that kind was reserved for those with rank and privilege on other worlds. So for Kevin, it was suck it up and spend long hours doing menial labor, sit home and starve, or . . .

It began with aptitude assessments to determine how a candidate might be of maximum service. On the physical tests, Kevin failed miserably, to the point that he thought they'd reject him on the spot. Even though the Armada was rumored to have a rejection rate of zero.

However, his proctor's face went slack with disbelief when he finished the math and logic modules in a fraction of the allotted time. They'd even given him a signing bonus (ten thousand in bit-gold) along with a letter of recommendation for a research and development post in the prestigious outer realm. He'd have to go through standard training, of course. A mere formality. Then he'd trade in his body armor for a mug of strong coffee. In fact, his biggest venture would be the walk from his workstation to the break room.

That's what they kept telling Kevin right up until the moment they assigned him to this warship. *We need bodies for combat*, they said. That was the revised version of their story.

He'd spilled all of this personal history to Tonya during their first week onboard. Tonya! Even an attempt to make eye contact should have turned his brain to mush. Yet somehow, someway, for reasons Kevin couldn't fathom, she had the opposite effect on him. Her mere presence was like a truth serum, loosening his tongue and causing him to dump his thoughts out for inspection. Well, most of them.

And here she was in the hangar—actually touching him! —this drop-dead gorgeous girl with easy charisma and sex appeal. She unlocked Kevin's face shield and raised it so that they were face-to-face. "I know what you're up to," she said. "And I get it." Her flirtatious gleam had vanished. She looked earnest and serious. A bronzed goddess of empathy.

Kevin felt his face redden. Tonya had come down here to rescue him, apparently. Because she was a friend, and she was protective of him.

Not that he could ask for a better bodyguard. In hand-to-hand combat drills, she was top in their unit. None of the men relished the prospect of locking up with her—not on the mat in the gym, anyhow.

Kevin felt desire and awe whenever he watched her in

action. Particularly the calmness in her face. She could have a two-hundred-pound man trying to take her head off and her expression remained as placid as it was at this moment. And while he had no way or proving it one way or another, Kevin often sensed that she was toying with her opponent, that she could render anybody on this warship unconscious in a skinny minute, including their drill instructors.

And now his silly escape attempt was done. Over. Finito. Tonya was about to take him by the hand and escort him back to his quarters like a little lost boy. At least that's what Kevin anticipated as he dropped his eyes from her steady gaze.

She lifted his chin, forcing his eyes to meet hers. "You're doing the right thing," she said. "You don't belong here. And they should know that. Idiots! You have a gift. It takes a special kind of person to sit by himself and not only problem solve but create. To them, you're just another warm body."

Kevin stood straighter. Tonya had that effect on him. Likely, he was just feeling the heat she gave off and attributing it to himself. But beggars couldn't be choosers. Kevin would take what he could get.

"If that's their value system, they don't deserve a man of your talents," Tonya said.

Kevin nodded, even though he'd never considered himself *too good* for the Armada. His exit plan had nothing to do with retribution or elevating his own station. He was simply fleeing a situation that he couldn't deal with even with Tonya babysitting him every step of the way.

Then he looked across the hangar at the closed hatch. It might as well be a million miles away. He forced himself to look at Tonya, hating himself for exposing even more of his weakness to her. "I can't do it," he said.

Tonya's generous mouth tumbled open as she smiled that easy smile of hers. She touched his face. The black glove on her hand left a sweet aftertaste on Kevin's lips. "We'll do it together," she said.

"But I can't let you go AWOL," Kevin protested. Not that he could stop her from doing anything.

"Not me," Tonya said. "You. We'll get you out of here, and they'll have no clue where to find you."

"But—"

"What you really need is someone to close the hatch doors when you leave," Tonya said.

She had a point. If the ship's scanners picked up an unexpected blip...way better if the hangar doors were closed. Something Kevin wouldn't be able to do from a launched vessel due to security protocol.

Her fingers encircled his right wrist. "C'mon, Kevin. You've got the power, dude."

His pulse hammering into the deafening silence, Kevin stood breathless as Tonya pressed his hand against the palm reader. He imagined a real shock to his fingertips. Silly. Because the glove emitted no electrical current. Nanotubes embedded in the glove read the wearer's DNA and generated an encrypted code for the palm reader to evaluate. A double authentication protocol that was both glove and wearer specific. Kevin hoped he'd mimicked it successfully.

The red circle on the reader turned green, indicating a big thumbs-up.

"Your chariot awaits, sir," Tonya said. She offered up a playful faux curtsy.

Well, yeah. He'd programmed the glove for elite-level clearance. That enabled unfettered access to anything in the hangar, including permission to pilot any of its vessels.

Even though he'd never actually flown before. This was not shaping up to be a good plan.

Tonya reassured him. "Hey. You've got this," she said. "You're going to Innes. Right?"

Kevin nodded. The Innes sector was a short jaunt from here—important because he had no food or provisions. It was also neutral territory beyond the jurisdiction of the Armada and every other faction. An equal opportunity offender, there was no extradition from Innes. Consequently, the entire sector had gotten a reputation as a haven for outlaws. However, Kevin just needed to buy some time to put together a new identity and figure things out.

"You don't have to know how to fly a hawker," Tonya said. "Just download your course map and let autopilot do all the work."

"What about when I get there?" Kevin said. This was a hell of a time to be asking questions like these.

"The hawker will just disengage in the general vicinity and float in orbit. No problem. A barge or a space station will see that baby and drool. They'll tow you in no questions asked. They'll probably take your ship as payment for their services, but you don't know how to fly it anyhow. So what the hey!"

Tonya leaned in and kissed him full on the lips, making the hair on the back of his neck stand up.

"You've got this, Kevin." She gave his hand a reassuring squeeze.

"You've got this."

THREE

The sound of the hangar doors whooshing open made Kevin's crotch draw up into his abdomen. This was like the start of a wild carnival ride, when you knew you'd made a mistake buying a ticket. Too late to turn back now. You could only hope to make it out in one piece. And not puking all over yourself would be an added bonus.

There were no safety restraints in the cockpit. Kevin's body armor adhered itself to the bucket seat. The dark windshield had closed over him, allowing him a view from every conceivable angle. However, the holographic touch-screen would be far more reliable for monitoring his surroundings.

Monitoring being the operative word in this case. The onboard computer was doing the actual flying. Kevin was a mere passenger. His weapon was stowed behind the seat within reach. Hence the expression, *riding shotgun.*

He didn't realize he was space-bound at first. He was waiting for a g-force kind of pressure. Something slamming him into his seat. But it was as if the hawker was stationary and the scenery shifted around it. The hangar disappeared, suddenly replaced by stars and darkness.

Kevin licked his lips, the taste of Tonya's kiss still lingering. She was right. He had this. Hell, he'd just outsmarted the Armada. How cool was that? Maybe they'd think twice about treating personnel like livestock in the future. Probably not. But one horse had sure as hell broken out of the corral.

With much of his angst at bay now, he reflected on how he'd pulled this off and laughed out loud in the empty cockpit.

New recruits were allowed a small amount of personal tech, all subject to screening, of course. Things like family holograms, books, music, and a few games like chess and poker.

And all executable programs were formatted with a specific data structure to allow the computer to find, parse, read, and run them. It was all about storing and retrieving data using pattern matching.

Kevin's Throwdown game, book reader, and slideshow all had innocuous header data. Armada AI had scanned them for malware and found nothing. But Throwdown, a space dogfight game, tied it all together. The game itself was dull, void of cool scenery and storylines. Just two ships fighting it out on a black background with a few distant stars thrown in for looks. Tonya always blew him up with ridiculous ease when they played it together.

Once the game launched, however, the seemingly random stars in the background formed a pattern of coordinates that served as a template. Using this template, Throwdown touched (but did not execute or launch) photo, books, and poker executables, pulling in partial instructions from each of them. The result was a worm built from bits and pieces of each. As the players duked it out on a cheesy star field, it compiled and launched itself into the network.

The worm didn't do any damage. A smart virus didn't kill its host, after all. Didn't eat data. Didn't touch a damn thing. All it did was pry and look. And giving Kevin kernel-level access was like throwing chickens into a fox's den.

Still savoring his victory, he checked the rear camera and watched the warship disappear from visual range. He wasn't totally in the clear yet—but the being out of sight produced a heady sense of liberation. Already, he'd dared to venture far beyond his courage level. All because Tonya had shown up at the last minute and talked him into it.

THE HAWKER PICKED UP SPEED, a fast acceleration that pressed Kevin hard against his seat. His stomach lurched. After all, he was putting his life in the hands of the onboard computer. All he could do was sit and wait.

Closing his eyes, Kevin concentrated on slow, steady breathing. The pressure of the seat against his back began to feel more inviting, and he began to find a sense of security in the inertia that held him in place. This was cruising speed. A far cry from full throttle, better known as *balls to the wall*.

He opened his eyes and gazed at the distant stars in the black beyond. Somewhere out there, the first jump was waiting. And it was up to his ship's navigation system to find and traverse it.

Still, he needed to at least stay somewhat engaged, even as a focused bystander. It was way too early to check his progress. But he pulled up the holographic map just the same. *Never too soon to start preparing.* That was something the drill instructors loved to yell as they jarred recruits out of deep slumber.

Kevin studied the 3D representation of his projected course and identified his current location by the blinking orb that didn't seem to be moving. It was going to be a long journey. Monitoring his progress was going to be a lot like watching metal rust.

The map would morph into new shapes and patterns based on his location. There were no compass points in deep space. No concept of longitude or latitude, north or south. Not even up or down. This was computer-based interpretation of *were, are,* and *would be.* And a single-person hawker's computer could only handle one iteration at a time.

He licked his lips again and thought of Tonya. Not a smart thing to do while careening through open space. On the other hand, no further action was required of him. At least not for a good long while. Still, shit happened sometimes. What shit, Kevin couldn't say. But he at least needed to quit dreaming and stay completely awake. With all of that in mind, Kevin resolved to remain alert—but at the same time, allow his emotional mainspring to unwind a little.

Approaching Jump Sector 1XQ-to-3AP.

Kevin almost wet his pants when he heard that system prompt and saw it flashing on the map. That meant he was coming up on the first of two wormholes. All according to plan. Except: he thought he'd reached this first wormhole way too soon.

Or maybe not. After all, he was nervous and uptight, his thoughts bouncing in a hundred different directions. And nobody could keep time in his own head. That's why time-keeping devices had been invented in the first place. Well, duh! All he had to do was look at the time elapsed. Almost half an hour. Or for his needs: fifteen hundred and eleven seconds and counting—it had to be that granular.

Kevin ran some of the math through his head. (He'd always been able to solve complex equations without a calculator, to the disdain of his classmates, which had led to more than a little bullying.) Based on his calculations, maybe he'd gotten here too soon. Maybe not. *Real conclusive,* he thought in disgust.

Actually, he *could* conclude that his arrival time was in the realm of reasonable expectation. Course maps were, after all, based on spatial relationships between faraway objects: warships, planets, wormholes, entire galaxies. And nothing stood still. Which required the mapping algorithm to make incessant adjustments. *Deviation shift* was the technical term. And course mapping handled that without issue.

Okay. So nothing to panic over. Yet the nagging voice in the back of Kevin's brain persisted. Call it instinct, call it paranoid. His gut—in fact, the very marrow of his being—insisted that something was amiss.

That sector identifier also gave him pause. *1XQ-to-3AP.* Probably no big deal. Software developers were often gearheads that overengineered everything to the nth degree. They couldn't even count to eleven without dropping their pants. Why simply count two wormholes using integer values 1 and 2 when you could come up with a hash code to make yourself look smart?

Then again...

Well, it couldn't hurt to check. In other words, don't trust what the map is telling you. Go one step further than just reading the heading labeled *Innes* that floated reassuringly above the holograph. That meant paging forward through the map itself, all the way to the final destination.

Which would bog things down a bit. Quantum brain farms on a warship or space station could churn through the map data without breaking a sweat. But a hawker's computer was going to struggle. One reason why pilots had restricted access—why they weren't allowed to monkey with things like this.

A fire burned in Kevin's chest. He was under no such restriction!

But when he placed his glove on the palm reader to invoke his elite access, a telltale beep sounded. Access denied.

No. It had to work. He'd given himself root-level privileges. Generals couldn't get at the shit he could. But no. It was shutting him out. He pressed down again in vain, still getting the same *Invalid User* response.

Tonya!

She'd squeezed his hand while she kissed him. Just a quick firm grip. And, of course, he'd been working with limited supplies, so this glove he'd made to circumvent system security didn't have the reinforced microfiber of a true battle-ready glove. Tonya had busted his nanotube seam, goddammit! She'd set him up. He wasn't a passenger. Or even cargo. He was a prisoner—stuck on this course to who-knew-where, and there wasn't a thing he could do about it.

There was one hope. The computer had allowed him to pull up the hologram of his current route. That implied that anybody sitting in that pilot's seat had at least minimal access. Hell, he could probably read books or play games on his way to wherever he was really going if nothing else.

Kevin queried his personal account. Nothing doing. Tonya had locked him out.

But this vanilla pilot account. Maybe it had access to his

personal tech. After all, it wasn't locked down. He knew the program ID of Throwdown. If he could force terminal-level access...

Kevin pulled up a virtual keypad and typed furiously. Yes. He was in. Well, not really. He could launch his worm-building apps. But doing that was all too little too late. It took hours for the worm to make inroads once the build occurred.

There had to be another way—there always was.

If only he had time...

ALSO BY BONNER LITCHFIELD

Science Fiction

Space Hack

Splicers

Let Bygones Be Bygones

Five Stories

Crime/Thriller

Long Day For Ray

Lunch Money

Stained Glass

ABOUT THE AUTHOR

Bonner Litchfield sold his first story in 2009 and never looked back.

Merging his years in software development with an inexhaustible supply of ideas, he writes in multiple genres with a focus on science fiction and thriller.

Bonner lives in North Carolina with a very patient wife and a dog who thinks he's one of the great minds of the 21st century.

When not writing, he enjoys running, CrossFit, reading, travel, and (of course!) cheesy TV shows.

Visit him at <u>bonnerlitchfield.com</u>

www.ingramcontent.com/pod-product-compliance
Lightning Source LLC
Chambersburg PA
CBHW031545310726
48971CB00008B/2626